WHEN ALL IS SAID AND DONE

When All Is Said and Done

Robert Hill

Graywolf Press
SAINT PAUL, MINNESOTA

Publication of this volume is made possible in part by a grant provided by the Minnesota State Arts Board, through an appropriation by the Minnesota State Legislature; a grant from the Wells Fargo Foundation Minnesota; and a grant from the National Endowment for the Arts, which believes that a great nation deserves great art. Significant support has also been provided by the Bush Foundation; Target; the McKnight Foundation; and other generous contributions from foundations, corporations, and individuals. To these organizations and individuals we offer our heartfelt thanks.

Supported by the Jerome Foundation in celebration of the Jerome Hill Centennial and in recognition of the valuable culture contributions of artists to society.

Published by Graywolf Press
2402 University Avenue, Suite 203
Saint Paul, Minnesota 55114
All rights reserved.

www.graywolfpress.org

Published in the United States of America

ISBN 978-1-55597-442-8 (cloth)
ISBN 978-1-55597-494-7 (paper)

2 4 6 8 9 7 5 3 1

Library of Congress Control Number: 2007925192

Cover design: Kyle G. Hunter

Cover art: © Veer

For my parents

ACKNOWLEDGMENTS

My gratitude to the following: Tom Spanbauer and the Dangerous Writers for constant inspiration; Liz Scott, Ellen Kesend, and Lily Gardner-Butts for getting me there; Neil Olson for patiently finding me a home; Fiona McCrae and everyone at Graywolf for making me feel so welcome; Literary Arts / Oregon Literary Fellowships and the Walt Morey Fellowship for their generosity; Mary Jaeger and Jerry Walker for an abundance of food and friendship; Glyn O'Malley for encouragement beyond measure; and John Azzopardi, for reminding me of the possibility of happy endings.

WHEN ALL IS SAID AND DONE

ONE

Take a deep breath.

𝓗AD THE NEW NURSE NOT GROWN UP NEXT TO
train tracks and not learned to sleep through derail-
ments, and had she been the third nurse of the six and
counting, the one who had the harelip and the stiff back
and who never could find a comfortable sleeping position, face down, or, God forbid, face up, then it would
not have been I who awakened and rattled like the Third
Avenue El past the diaper pail and the stuffed animals
and the high chair and the rocking horse and the playpen and the layette, in the dark, in the middle of last
night, in the middle of cloudy, moonless last night, to
find out why the baby was crying and if it was the feed-
me cry or the change-me cry or the cry that necessitates
Vaseline and the rectal thermometer with the mysterious

black speck in the mercury; and had I not made sure to make Dan make sure to make Macy's make sure to put the extra-large brass casters on the legs of the crib so that the crib could roll over the extension cord to the reading lamp by the chair with the coats on it and over the braided rug in the living room/dining room/nursery without catching, then my big toe would not have collided with one of them, and I wouldn't have slapped the mobile attached to the crib and the yellow horse and the green elephant would not have found themselves in an embrace Mother Nature never intended, and the baby—the baby!—wouldn't have been so startled and screamed a scream that is now yet another scream I have to learn in order to tell the parade of nurses how to respond to it, since I'm really no good at it, and the baby's much better off in their sometimes capable hands; and had I not tried to climb over the bassinet to wring that still-sleeping nurse's boxcar-thick neck for not waking up I wouldn't have tripped over Spock and the Nurses Registry Directory and stubbed my other big toe; and as I am sure is obvious to anyone with the slightest shred of good sense, I would not have been wearing open-toed shoes this morning—open toes that, as you can see, are giving my swollen big toes room to swell more;

and I certainly would never have darted into DePinna's of all places on my way to the office to buy new stockings to replace the ones I started the day with which my swollen toes tore and which then soaked through anyway in the rainstorm that I should have anticipated what with last night's moon-obscuring cloud cover; and had I not needed to switch to the gray lizard handbag to go with these gray lizard open toes that need new heel crowns come to think of it, then the salesgirl in hosiery would not have whispered through her insufficiently bleached mustache that really could have used plucking that I had lipstick on my tooth, and had she not, I would not have pulled out the mirror in the black velvet pouch in the zippered compact sleeve to check, and I would not have found the business card stuck to the back of the mirror in the velvet pouch in the zippered compact sleeve that I must have put there so that I would remember to retrieve it, the business card Clifton had his secretary give me one morning months ago after a night not all that dissimilar to last night, save that it involved Dan's elbow, the hat rack, and the nurse-of-the-moment's trachea, yet, which, thankfully, did not require a complete wardrobe shift, at least, not for me, the business card for the realtor in Connecticut Clifton and Celeste used when it dawned on her that a six-room duplex on Central Park West was not high life enough; and, well, to make a long story short, had it not been for the crowded apartment and the crying baby and the stubbed toes that I had just had pedicured and the nurse whose replacement comes tomorrow and the gray lizard open toes and the soggy hose and the changed handbag and that poorly depilatoried DePinna's girl and the lipstick and the mirror, I would not have found the card and I would not have called Charmington Country Real Estate in Charmington, Connecticut, and I would not have spoken with a Mrs. Giselle Jeanteau Cadoux St. Montpellier who's about as French as that debutante who's marrying that senator, and I would not have had the conversation that sent me over the edge and straight through the doors at Hattie Carnegie this afternoon for the well-deserved consoling of this sheerling beret that I've had my eye on for weeks but hadn't dared to indulge myself with before, and now I see I should have because it works so well with the bag and the shoes and what difference will one more hatbox make in that tiny apartment now anyway?

Insane? Perhaps. I'd think the same thing if it were anybody else but me.

I just wanted something to go right today, doesn't anybody understand that?

When I found that business card I thought good! yes! marvelous! I'll call! And so I called. I called Charmington Country Real Estate. I didn't even need to look at the card when the operator picked up. Charmington 6-0497, I said without blinking, it's only two digits away from the baby's Social Security number and if you flip the 4 and the 7 it's the address my sister lived at right after her divorce.

I called. I got that woman. That woman! With all those names! I'm amazed that I even remembered them, that I was able to contort my tongue to pronounce them all properly.

I told her how I'd heard of Charmington. A colleague of mine recommended it, I said. It and you, her, I said. He gave me your card, her card, I said. I wanted to say the card with so many names on it, but I didn't want to scotch anything, make fun of anything. I wanted it all to start clean and fresh like lace from a nunnery. You'd she'd been so helpful to his wife I said he said and said she said so too, his wife, I mean, they said to me about her, I told her.

She was intrigued. A colleague you say, she said. And whom might that be, she said. She sounded genuinely flattered that her reputation had sashayed down the Merritt Parkway and thrown its nickel into the Greenwich toll basket. Had I been she, I would have been curious to know whether it had proceeded east to the FDR or west to the Henry Hudson, but she sounded like the type that's only ever been into the city to see *Oklahoma!* At matinee. With boots on.

And mind you, I said colleague intentionally. I didn't want her to think that I was just a housewife calling on her husband's behalf. I wanted her to know that I had as much authority to make that call as Dan.

Why should I lie?

I had the card. Clifton gave it to me, not Dan. I told her Clifton Park, Clifton and his wife Sunny, I said. Well, actually, I said she probably only knew her as Celeste Park. I didn't mean anything by it.

It's not as if she and I, Celeste, Sunny, Mrs. Clifton Park and I are bosom buddies: we're civil, Clifton does sign my paychecks after all. Once in a while, I'm social with the both of them in the city, when Clifton insists she join and she hasn't something with her snotty friends planned. How do I know who calls her Celeste and who calls her Sunny and who calls her that infantile Su-Su like she's still a Gamma Phi at Pembroke.

I wasn't trying to lord anything over her. I said a name. A name. I didn't say they've seen me off on the RMS Caronia. I didn't say we've lunched at Lutece, which is getting harder and harder to get into. I certainly didn't tell her she'd probably come in one of those Claire McCardell housedressy things with the matching oven mitts.

Oh, she said. Her voice sounded so bright, it caught me off guard, like an apology before you're even aware of the offense. I'm sure in person that oh would have meant let me have your coat and wouldn't you like to sit here by the fireplace and that hat is darling with those shoes and that bag and what do you take in your coffee. Clifton and his wife Sunny, I say, whom she probably knows as Celeste, I say, and she says Su-SuParkwhata-delightsheiswe'vebecomethebestoffriends.

She says don't I just adore Clifton and Su-Su's Greek Revival on Ye Olde Uppercrestridgesummit Lane. She says wasn't that a delightful cocktail party they hosted two Saturdays ago for the Gabriel von Aufterheids. She says how silly of her to be telling me things I already know when we were there weren't we oh how sorry she is that she hadn't a chance to make our acquaintance and how so like Su-Su not to introduce us, isn't it wasn't it mightn't it not be?

No, I said. Actually, we couldn't make it. It was Passover.

Oh? she said. Then she paused. It was so slight, I thought maybe I'd missed something lighting my cigarette. It was just a catch of a pause, something out of the corner of her throat.

Oh, she said again, she finally said, again.

Low in her throat.

Stretched out.

Disappearing over the horizon.

Oh.

That terrible kind of oh. That your name is on a list oh. That would you step in here a moment please oh.

You're Mrs., she said, the same way she said oh.

That's me, I said, all Pepsodent smile to a pigeon gnawing at her baby's talon on the window ledge. Her turn of tone surprised me, but I've encountered it before, in conference rooms full of stiff-suited men who act as though I should be there in my girdle to clean up after their meetings, not lead them. I just ignore them and pretend there's nothing wrong and I dazzle and I sparkle and I glitter and I shine and I win them over justlikethat. If my son learns anything from me, it'll be how to do that, to a room, a town, a club. Ignore, dazzle, and triumph. Madame would be no different, I thought.

I thought.

You work for Mr. Park, she said. Disappearing voice.

Clifton, I wanted to correct her. Clifton.

Bookkeeper, she says. Not a question even.

Executive, I say. A little hot. Had to remove an earring. Still, not too.

And your husband, she says.

Sales, I say.

Rugs or something, she says.

Rugs? Textiles, I tell her.

I don't know where she got rugs.

Financing an issue, she says, or no?

We're good to go, I tell her.

But it was already too late.

Anybody could see that.

I should have seen it.

From the city, she says. Like it's a dare. Like she's daring me to lie and say my stole is mink when we both know it's nutria.

And it's in me like a flash fire, like an ink stain.

Brooklyn, I said. Brooklyn, that's what she wanted to hear, not Manhattan, no, nobody's getting out of

Brooklyn this year except the Dodgers, are they. No, not this year, not any year soon. I spat it out I might as well have been spraying saliva saying *shaitel* and *shtetl* and *shabbes* candles. I might as well have been my grandmother throwing her fits in Yiddish, those embarrassing fits, so King's Highway.

What good would it do to explain that I'd fled that crowded two-family on Tompkins Avenue years ago, that old house full of women who couldn't wait to be widows, giving in to their dowagers' humps and their sagging breasts and their segregated shuls and their liver spots and their orthopedic shoes and their police whistles and their shattered dreams, that I'd crossed the bridge when the troop ships came home and I found a man who wanted me—me—and I moved straight from my mother's bedroom into his without smashing any glass under any Huppa, didn't I care about my virginity they all shried that was the last thing I was worried about shedding.

Then she had the gall to say it, not actually say it say it, but intimate it say it, you know? I don't believe you'd be very happy in Charmington, she said, all Grace Kelly, all French Riviera, this Giselle Jeanteau Cadoux St. Montpellier Vichy sympathizer.

Oh, I said, and why is that?

Just a hunch, she says.

A hunch. Six million and she suspects mice in the basement.

Tell me something, I said. Is Smarmyngton a restricted community?

And she tittered.

Ha ha ha ha.

Just like that. I kid you not.

Not at all, she said. It's just that you'd be the first, she said. And who really wants to be the first of anything, she said, unless you're a Lindbergh?

A Lindbergh.

Clever of her, no? His position before the war? Really, very clever of her, I have to hand it to her. Saying it without saying it. Probably smoothing her leiderhosen as she said it.

Ardsley, Armonk, Scarsdale, Rye. I've referred people to those towns, she said. People from the city. People like you, she said. Can you believe that? Perfectly nice towns, she said. And the trains go there.

Matthausen, Bergen-Belsen, Treblinka. Little Levittown barracks communities and the trains went there, too, I said.

She didn't care.

Shame our paths won't cross, she said. Su-Su says you're such a smart dresser, too. Never a thread out of place she says. Always dressed to the nines she says. Your armor, she calls it. That Su-su. I could see her blue eyes glow like a bottle of toilet water on that one.

Yes, that Su-Su. What the hell is that all about? My armor. Thin as a martini-glass stem she is that Su-Su. New Look? She never heard of it. Try No Look.

I can refer you to another real estate professional, she said, a colleague.

No, Frenchie, that wouldn't be necessary, I may have said, or said something similar. All I know is I was standing at this point. My toes throbbing. Throbbing. Knocked the chair smack into the filing cabinet. Scared the pigeons off the ledge even.

And then she wished me well. Giselle Jeanteau Cadoux St. Montpellier goose-stepped through her Emily Post for tips on Polite Contempt and Socially Acceptable Kiss-Offs. I'm sure you'll be very happy wherever you end up, she said, brisk, perfunctory, like a teacher who's betting there won't be much of anything next to your name in the yearbook but has to say something.

Wherever I end up. Like I'm a dog, a cur. What, a German shepherd?

I wanted to slam the phone down. I wanted to break an eardrum. I was squeezing the receiver with such force that the veins in my hand stretched the freckles so wide they looked like dotted swiss.

And then she said, as if she hadn't said enough already, as if she hadn't kept me on the phone for so long that now I'd have to get a cab it was raining so hard and my open toes would be ruined thirty-five dollars down the drain, she said oh, oh, Mrs., before you go, I do want to say how sorry I am.

For poodle skirts, I said.

For your loss, she said.

My what, I said. My what?

Su-Su told me, she said.

I couldn't for the life of me imagine what else Su-Su told her about me.

My age? Where I hide my good jewelry? What?

And then it hit me.

Su-Su told her. Her good friend Su-Su told her. Her bestoffriendsSu-Su told her what she had no business telling her. Only half of what she had no business telling her, truth to tell. So she hadn't shared so much as cooking sherry with the Gabriel von Aufterheids at the Park's Reichstag Revival on Ye Olde Wolf's Lair, had she?

You haven't spoken with Sunny for some time, I take

it, or you would know what you were talking about, I said, because even Mrs. Park would have told you, I said.

I don't understand, she said.

Do you mean? she said.

Yes, I said.

He lived.

He? she said.

A boy? she said.

He lived?

Yes, I said. He lived, I said. He's alive, I said. He was alive all the time, I said. He was very small and there was too much fluid and they couldn't hear his heartbeat.

Oh, she said.

Oh, oh, oh, she said,

What a blessing, she said. And then, after a moment, such a long moment, what a blessing for you and your husband, she said.

Yes, I said, unable to keep my shoulders from dropping into the word, my anger from falling off me like a stretched stocking. The way she said blessing. Out of nowhere. I pulled the chair back and fell into it the way you would after climbing five flights. Something in the way she said blessing. You'd think it was *Mazeltov*, a weary *Mazeltov*. From a stranger. This stranger. I could feel crescent moons of tears pooling on my lower lashes. Yes, I said. Yes it was. It is, I said. I had to tilt my face to the blotter or my mascara would have streaked my cheeks like a Japanese watercolor. It's surprising how loud teardrops are when they've got something hard to hit.

On the other end, little choked inhales, little watery baby breaths.

She said, I wasn't so blessed, I lost mine, and I can't have more.

Oh, I thought.

Oh, oh, oh, I thought.

That poor woman, I thought. She lost hers and said she can't have more. And what she means is she can't have any, ever. And maybe that's why she had to say it the way she said it, fast, like she was running for a train, forcing it all out in a single breath.

I held mine waiting for her to catch hers.

I think she must have put her hand over the mouthpiece, she was crying full-out, I could tell, but it sounded muffled in cotton. Every once in a while I'd catch one good loud sob when she'd have to have fanned her fingertips under her eyes to splay the tears.

I was leaning on the desk with the receiver away from my mouth, listening, just listening to her cry, her priest hearing her confession. The pigeon and her baby floated back onto the window ledge they were so quiet about it, no spastic seizures of shaking the rain off their feathers, no claw clicks, not a coo, not so much as a feathertip tapping the glass.

They joined me in that suspended state patiently listening to her sobs, to her staccato sobs, hand on, hand off, hand on, hand off. It wasn't until my bracelet scraped the desktop that I realized just how quiet I was being, that the charms on it tinkled as I tilted the baby's picture away from the lamp glare, the picture I gave everyone, his first studio shot, the one in which he's wearing the gray flannel jumper and the little bow tie and the white shirt with the Peter Pan collar and that baby-bird smile of his.

I hadn't the heart to tell Giselle of the miracle she herself was cheated out of. That he weighed a single pound. That he fit in the palm of the nurse's hand. That he was so early his fingernails hadn't formed. That the doctor, for all his Harvard diplomas, kept muttering over and over my God, my God. I hadn't the heart to paint for her that he looked like a diapered puppy the six weeks he lived in that glass box, hatching like a chick in a brooder, his hands bandaged and bound in what looked like baby boxing gloves so he wouldn't wrench the tubes from his nose and mouth.

How do you explain to someone that you can feel gratitude, that I felt it, like I've never felt it before, as real and as visceral a sensation as the ache in my loins that lasted long after delivery, gratitude for the thick rubber gloves attached to incubators, matinee-length I thought the first time I inched my hands into them. Those black, black gloves, not at all like mine today, so tender the gray kid. Those oil-slick black, cold, antiseptic fingers caressing his tiny wrinkles. That was my son's—my son's—first sensation of me and thank God for it.

Poor Giselle. Did her own mother rest a reassuring palm on her wrist the way mine did, saying if there's one prayer, one prayer in a million that the doctors are wrong, then kaynahorah that's the prayer you believe in? And what if she did, and what if mine had, and what if that hope of hopes wasn't enough, and how do you go on living when it isn't enough, when you've convinced yourself that only the miraculous can happen, that only the improbable can come true? I don't know what I would do if after all that time and all that hoping for the best and all those hours that I read the stretch marks on my belly like they were tea leaves foretelling only happy times, like they were an atlas with only one route pointing me to paradise, if after all of that, all of that, he didn't live, I couldn't live, I wouldn't want to live, I don't know how she lived, how does anyone live past the death of a baby?

What good is talk of miracles and gratitude and prayers and houses and deeds and mortgages and property lines and neighborhoods and schools and sweet little breakfast nooks when there's no high chair to draw to the table?

I wanted to say but you can adopt, surely you've thought of it, surely she had considered it, hadn't she? Did her not doing so have something to do with her husband, his pride, a family objection to interrupted lineage? I could ask her, she was vulnerable enough to confide, but it seemed cruel somehow, moving in for her Achilles' heel. Which husband fathered the child she doesn't have? Is that why she has all those last names? Do all those men long for children she's unable to conceive?

I couldn't. Even I couldn't. Instead, I said how sorry I was, how truly sorry I was for her loss. It was all I could say. It really was. It was all I could.

Thank you, she said. Thank you for that, she said.

Her palm was gone from the mouthpiece, her tears, if they still were coming, were a trickle. And then she blew her nose. Actually blew her nose right into the phone. The pigeons swiveled their heads toward me, that's how loud it was. Maybe not that loud but picture me doing a full Lucy Ricardo reaction to it, it was loud.

Still. Anyway. So.

How I hate sad phone calls. They're so hard to disconnect, harder when they're between strangers. You can't end with I'll see you soon.

Well, I said, breathing it out like the last of a tire's air.

Listen, she said, her voice strong like it was at the beginning, but without that sales lacquer sprayed on it, listen, before you go, she said, there are towns farther north, she said, wonderful towns, artists colonies really, she said, with famous residents even, writers and actors and publishing and advertising and all sorts of creative types, she said, so much more interesting than Charmington, she said, so much better for children, although don't quote me on that, she said, and coughed a small laugh, and I echoed it.

I echoed it, but not because I appreciated the joke, mind you. I beg your pardon, I said.

Eastport, Eastland, Eastbrook, Eastly. I can put you

in touch with a very nice gentleman, a colleague whom I'm sure you'd like, she said, a Mr. Ernst Schmidt, she said, well actually, she said, I think he now goes professionally by the name Ernie Smith, she said. Shall I call Mr. Schmidt, Mr. Smith for you and have him give you a call? she said, save you the bother of having to track him down?

I don't understand, I said. I really didn't. I still do not, not really.

You mean? I said.

I'd be happy to, she said.

You'll refer us? I said.

It's the least I can do, she said.

And he'll call us? I said.

Tonight, at home, she said, unless that would be inconvenient, what with, well, the baby and all, she said, walking that precipice, without tears, good for her.

That would be so nice, I said. Thank you, I said. I meant it, too. I said, thank you, I even went so far as to say thank you, Giselle, although I wasn't too sure that I should or moreover wanted to further the intimacy between us, our conversation had turned surprisingly intimate, yes, but hardly first-name cozy, I followed it up with Mrs. St. Montpellier.

Oh, she said, nobody calls me that anymore, she said, and tittered her ha ha ha ha this time with the sincere embarrassment of a schoolgirl caught in the merest slip of a white lie. It's Mrs. La Grevesnes, she said. Two S's, one's silent, she said. I just got married.

Again, I thought. That's how she goes on. That's how she lives beyond her loss, I thought. And another French man, to boot. Where does she find all these French men, I wondered. Do we have a French Embassy in Charmington I wanted to ask, but the call was expensive enough and too late to reverse the charges. Clifton would be livid, I thought, livid but what of it, if Sunny hadn't blabbed Giselle wouldn't have blubbered, he should pay for it.

I congratulated her and wished her well and adjusted my one and only wedding ring and we said our goodbyes and that was that.

Still raining out, not as much, less, a little; I can wait for the bus and save the taxi fare. My stockings should hold until I get home. Open toes, for crying out loud. Better put the new hat back in its box. I hate when fur gets damp. Where are my gloves?

I want to get home. I want to see the baby. I hope that girl has him in the plaid jumper like I told her. I'll undress, take off my makeup, shower, put on my new wool robe, the red one with the white collar, lay out my clothes for tomorrow, I think they said sunny but I'm not taking a chance, no open toes that's for sure, no way Jose, and while Dan cooks dinner, I'll sit with the baby in the rocker and I'll give him his bottle tonight. I'll say one thing for sleeping beauty, she knows how to warm his formula properly. I wonder if that man really is going to call tonight or if she was just being polite.

The new nurse is supposed to come tomorrow morning—that was a whole other phone call—the agency said 7:00 but those people never know anything, I better just double-check and make sure. If a new one doesn't show up, she doesn't show up, I'm not going to make myself crazy, the uniform fits this one I'll give her a second chance.

Giselle Jeanteau Cadoux St. Montpellier La Grevesnes *ici, votre nom.*

Oy.

TWO

Into the woods.

"ℋ ERE'S WHAT YOU DO," HE'S TELLING ME. "YOU
take Route 47 down to 118. 118 west over the 3 where
it T's with the rear alley to Satchel's. Stay on that till
you go by Good Knights Funeral Home. The sign isn't
there anymore, but it looks like that house in that movie
with what's-their-names. Just on the other side of where
they pulled up the tracks is Olde Trail Street. Well, it's
called something different now. Rench? Rinch? I don't
know, something Re. Anyway, so you turn left there. You
follow the blind curve back over the tracks. You might
want to honk your horn, you never know. They moved
a house there once. Fell off. Helluva mess. And at the
stop sign you'll see it—it'll be just on the other side
of Gloanestown Turnpike, opposite the lot where the

clock tower used to be. Can't miss it. Tell 'em I sent you. They'll fix you up nice."

———

I've been staring at leaves. I never owned a tree before and now I have more than I know what to do with. A week ago yesterday, the day we closed on the house, the place looked like the October page on the calendar the bank gave us, all ketchup and mustard against an Aqua Velva sky. Sunday we moved in. Diane hurricained Tuesday night. Blew every God-damned leaf off of every God-damned tree. Left the yard looking like coleslaw that had seen better days. I don't own a rake.

Neither does Ed Fence. Ed's our neighbor. Ed and his wife Mary and their six daughters, "all under the age of seven!" live in the four-bedroom "moderne" on the other side of the lane, downhill from my septic's leach field. Must have seen me out front with my dazed just-realized-I'm-standing-in-quicksand look. Must have struck him as as good a sign as any that now's a convenient time to be new neighborly. Startled me from behind. Thought I heard water, but turns out it was the Schlitz in his pockets. "I'd lend you mine if I owned one," he says, "but since I don't, can I interest you in a cold one?"

Something about Ed's breath makes me want to put some distance between us. It's not just the two-fisted tobacco and beer thing. Something hot and mulchy is going on in his gut, and the secret is out.

"A cold one, huh?" I say. It was only nine when I came out and I can't have been standing here all that long. I mean, come on.

"It's, uh, a little early for me," I say, making sure my smile is friendly. And I give him the wink so he'll know that A) I'm a drinking man, but B) I'm keeping it under control.

"I'll rain check you, then," Ed says, giving me the wink back that says A) I hear you, Mac, and yippee! B) That's more for me!

"I've been looking for a good liquor store," I say to him, even though what I really need is a good hardware store and, let's be frank here, a rake. But Ed's my new neighbor and I want to be polite, so whatever advice he can give me, I'll let him give me. "Any you can recommend?"

So this is when he directs me to McGruder's Wines & Spirits. I'd need a compass and an Indian guide to find the place even with his directions, but he doesn't need to know that.

"What about right up the road at that little shopping center?" I ask him. "No liquor store there?"

"Mmmmmm, yeah," he says, shaking his head side to side. From this I'm guessing that's a no, un-uh, bad idea. I take a stab at it.

"No? Un-uh? Bad idea?" I say.

He squints his eyes and bobs his head up and down like it's a lure teasing a trout.

"Yeah, no," he says, and the bobbing goes back to side to side like the trout decided to play. "Pricey," he says. "Used to go there." Says, "We run a high tab. You'd think they'd give us a break. Keep these people in business," he says, "and that's the thanks you get!"

That mulchy thing is worse the more emphatic his words. I have to sip air through the side of my mouth so I don't look to him like I smell shit on a shoe.

"Wife home?" he says, his eyes drifting in the general direction of my living-room windows but never coming to rest there.

I can't for the life of me imagine introducing him to her. I can just hear her say "good fences make good neighbors, huh?" a little too proud of the pun.

Ed's tall. A good six-feet-two, -three, at least. Tall and skinny, can't hide that no matter how bulky his coat is trying to make him look. My ankles fill a room more than his neck does. It's not all that cold out today, not really, yet his Adam's apple looks like a maraschino cherry and that bony nose and those sunken cheeks of his are as blood-shot as his eyes. Can't picture him on a bank calendar. He's got all his hair, though. I'll give him that.

———·———

There's a single green leaf on the maple just beyond Ed's head. One lone leaf, doing a lazy wave in the breeze, green except for a thread of jaundice running down its stem and spreading. Survived the storm by fending off fall I guess, but can't pretend it's summer forever. It'll be dead soon enough. Still, I appreciate it hanging on. Makes me smile to think it's doing me a favor.

Ed swivels his head to see what I'm smiling about. "See the cow?" he asks all excited. He could be rubber-necking over a crowd of heads watching the ball game in an appliance-store window the way he cranes to see what he hopes I'm seeing. I take the opportunity to step back from him a bit, not much but far enough to breathe in something other, anything other, than him, a cow even. Soon enough he realizes there is no cow round-ing third so he turns back to me and as he does swipes the air behind him, one of those disgusted go-on-get-outta-here swipes that clips the maple leaf and sends it spiraling. "Damn, I thought it was the cow," he says. For a second I think he finally smells his own breath the way his face torques, but it hits me he's reading the disappointment on my face as being about the cow and not about the leaf falling, stupid as being disappointed about either is. "Aw, give it time," he says, consoling me. "You'll see the cow. Wanders out of Gilford's pasture on the other side of the woods behind your place. All the time, just wanders out and comes through the woods and moseys down to the lane like it's looking for the late edition. Some sight. Wife'll get a kick out of it!"

Wanna bet?

My wife is six months pregnant. The way she swells up it looks like twelve.

Because of last time, we have to consider the possibility of something going wrong again. "It just won't," she usually says, like it's a refutation of the weather forecast, usually followed by her reaching for a cigarette and lighting it with more force than usual. "No, it won't," I usually confirm, all the while locking my sights on her match, on the lookout for the bit of sulfur shrapnel that usually flies free during these strike strike strikes.

Sometimes she says "Oh, God, Dan, what if . . ." and because her chin is usually trembling when she says this, something she doesn't usually allow anyone to see, I rake her into my arms and say very low and very soft "now, now . . . now, now," all the while thinking what if . . . what . . . if? She's six months pregnant and more nervous about it than either one of us'll admit she is. The last thing she needs is to learn we've moved onto a cattle crossing.

Crazy as it seems, I blame Fence for this. I really want that rake now.

I want to hit him with it.

Something tells me he and his wife never had any complications with their "six under seven!" I'm suddenly so angry by this thought, by both thoughts, by all of it: by Fence and the trespassing cow, by Fence and his wife and what I don't need a bookie to tell me were their six perfect pregnancies, angry about the leaf, angry about the no rake, angry about the useless directions to the cut-rate liquor store, even angry about Fence's full head of hair. On top of it all, I'm embarrassed that I'm angry. Jesus Christ if that doesn't beat all. And so busy being angry and embarrassed that I don't notice how light-headed I feel all of a sudden, that I'm dizzy and that

I've stopped breathing. I don't realize any of this until Fence's bony fingers are squeezing my shoulder like he's testing a God-damned cantaloupe. And his hand on me like that catches me by surprise so of course I gulp air and sure enough as soon as I do Fence lets loose with a really pungent "whoa there, neighbor!" and oh boy is that smell right there again running up my nose like it's got a hot date. The dizziness isn't from the smell, that I know 'cause I've been having it off and on for about four years now, who knows why, but the nausea sure as hell is. So I shake Fence's hand off me like it's a horsefly and I take a few more steps back and try to breathe in as much pure oxygen as possible before whatever it is that's dead in his gut pokes its mug out for another good look-around.

Leave, Fence. I want you to leave. I want you and your pockets full of now warm "cold ones" to slosh back where you came from. I don't want you meeting my wife any more than I want my wife to meet the cow. I'm thinking this as he gives me the look that says poor guy, one too many tours of duty, was it? So wouldn't you know I'm smiling back at him with all the proof he'd need to lock me in the VA's happy hut for the duration. How? How did I go from looking at leaves to looking like I need an extended leave?

I take a breath and exhale. I take another, let it out.

Fence takes one, takes two. Lets 'em both out. My way.

"So, um," I say.

"Um, yeah-h-h-h," Fence says.

———•———

For a few seconds, maybe a minute, two minutes tops, we're back to salvaging our best intentions, silently summing up the common green of our beings. Two grown men, husbands, fathers, veterans, homeowners, suburbanites, forest dwellers without a rake between us, neighbors standing a foul breath apart under a canopy of crisscrossed maple and tulip and hickory and oak and chestnut and walnut and sucker dogwood limbs. The elms are all gone. Blighted to oblivion. So are the Mohawks and the Cayugas and the Onondagas who once knew these woods cold. Must have faced the prospect of strange, new neighbors with the same mix of curiosity and anxiety and every whiff of feelings in between, only to retreat, then diminish, then perish, becoming little else than the mulch that Ed and I are standing on.

Like I said, the moment lasts a minute, two tops. What kills it, what bites my balls awake, is Myrmy screaming from inside the house. Loud, shrill, plate-glass smashes of screams that lock you stone-still a split second before you have to break the speed limit. Oh shit! Oh shit! Not the baby! I'm thinking on my way up the moss slope to the front door. Oh no! Not the baby! Oh shit! Oh no!

"Dan, Dan!" she's screaming. "Come quick! Dan, come quick!"

"I'm coming!" I holler mad through the wood and insulation and plaster. "I'm coming, Myrmy!"

"Dan! Oh, my God! Oh, my God!" she's screaming. There's real terror coming out of her. I'm scared. I've never heard anything like it.

"Dan, Dan, come quick!" she's screaming. "Oh, God, come quick!"

I'm just about to throw my whole body against the knob when I hear what I hoped to God I'd never hear.

"Dan!" she screams, "oh, God, Dan! There's a cow at the kitchen door!"

Goddamn! Godfuckingsonofabitch! This is what she's been screaming about?

"This is what you've been screaming about?" I say between pants.

I've run up that God-damned slope like I'm God-damned Red Grange, practically took the door off the God-damned hinges, clipped my kneecap on the God-damned packing crate full of nursery crap I asked that Margaret Hamilton look-alike nurse to move away from the God-damned front door and the baby's in his play-

pen in the living room mauling the bars and screaming
bloody murder like it's his last night on death row and
the nurse is leaning over him like a broken branch doing
semaphore with a teddy bear in one hand and a God-
damned rattle in the other like that's gonna calm him
down, all because little miss city girl's had a run in with
Elsie, not that you could tell, she's as composed as a Saks
Fifth God-damned Avenue maternity-wear illustration,
I want to say, but since I left a God-damned lung somewhere on the front steps I can't quite get it out.

She tsks, my wife, the cicada. "You ran up here. Oh,
I wish you hadn't!"

Now that I'm standing in one spot, well, doubled
over in one spot like a spent linebacker, trying to catch
my breath, and re-attach my knee, and get my heart to
knock off the Gene Krupa shit, I can tell that she's truly
grateful that I ran the forty for her regardless kid or cow
or what have you. She doesn't say a word, rarely does at a
moment like this. Instead, she takes a quick inventory of
her surroundings, and I dog her eyes all the way. Waring
blender, mixer, toaster, electric skillet, waffle iron. Check.
I follow her gaze up to the circular fluorescent bulb in
the light fixture, then down to the linoleum beneath her
loafers, then to me and I'm guessing my thinning lid and
the sweat that's shellacking it, then over to the dishrag

draped over the sink rim that she plucks up without a word, snaps open like a linen napkin, folds in half, pleats, and sets down on the counter in front of me the way a sympathetic bartender would serve me a stiff one.

Come to think of it, my own mother used to do the same thing, though with nowhere near the same flourish, when she'd hand a sweat rag to my father after she had him skittering up and down those apple trees behind the Dorchester house for those pies of hers.

And just like my own mother, Myrmy's doing her damnedest to hold back on some little social lesson, some little etiquette enhancement so that devotion can get its due. She's a good woman, she really is, never better than when she's corralling herself back into her own pen without any arched-eyebrow lasso from me.

Like right now she's not telling me to not use the back of my coat sleeve to wipe the sweat off my face, she's letting the rag say it for her. Nor is she hocking me about the leaves I tracked in. Or that I (probably) left the front door open.

She knows that I know like my father knew that she can't quite voice it and that I accept that she can't, so nothing needs to be said on either side. That's our compact. Ed and Mary Fence I'm sure have their own version, and I'd bet the farm that if you grilled any other

Mr. and Mrs. back to Adam and Eve they'd 'fess up something similar.

"Where's the cow?" I finally have the breath to say, trading sleeve for rag and sympathy for propriety, not to mention alarm for relief.

"Gone," she says.

"Where'd it go?"

"I haven't a clue."

"What was it doing?" I said.

"Standing."

"Where?"

"By the steps."

"Just standing?" I said.

"Yes. No."

"Then what?"

"It had its nose through the rail."

I said, "Why?"

She said, "It was sniffing the milk box."

"And . . . ?"

And nothing. She gives me the look that says give it up, brother.

"Let me get this straight," I say. "There was a cow. At the kitchen door. Sniffing the milk box. And now she's gone."

"Ye-e-e-s-s!" she says, like I'd just outfoxed Van

Doren on *Twenty-One*. When the baby reads his first "A" or "O" that yes is going to be deafening.

We could go another inning, we could go into overtime, I could look for hoofprints, but there's something fairy-tale-ish about the whole thing and maybe that's the point.

So I ask, "Did she run off with the fork and the spoon?"

Once again, she doesn't say anything. And once again, she doesn't have to. That she breaks into a smile bigger than her lipstick can cordon off is my little bit of Eden.

After, a moment.

"I'll go check the baby," I say. His sentence must have been commuted because his shrieks have softened to a misdemeanor.

She tsks, letting the bugs back into paradise. "Dora . . . !"

"Hilda."

"Hilda, can't you calm him?" she says to the living room, by way of the dining room, from here in the kitchen.

"I'll do it," I tell her. "You sit down."

"No, no," she says, cupping her belly with one hand

and waving me away with the other while doing her slow, pregnancy crab waddle out of the room. I wonder if it'll be that same hand, manicured, wedding-ringed and all, that'll wave me away in bed some night one day.

It's a good thing I truck after her 'cause just as she rounds the corner into the living room the front door creaks open a skosh more than almost-closed and Ed's hairy head springs through like a bushy jack-in-the-box. Myrmy gasps "who the . . . ?" and uses Hilda's shoulder as a mooring post, and Hilda gasps "what the . . . ?" and drops the rattle on the baby's hand, and the baby goes into his silent all-hell's-gonna-break-loose-anew windup, and I do a quick dodge and lunge between Myrmy and Hilda to scoop him up just in time for that new hell to do its number on my eardrum as I'm trying to say "Ed, this is my . . ." and Ed's finishing or finishing off my introduction with " . . . wife, yeah, glad to know ya! Hear you saw the cow!"

———

I was told that in the country, in the suburbs, out of the city, away from New York, far from East Fifty-seventh between First and Second, no longer down the block from a Chinese laundry and an Italian market and a

Polish butcher and a French bakery that you happen to love, nor up three flights plus stoop but down at ground level, more or less, a mile from the closest store, two miles from the parkway, eight miles from the train station, God only knows how many miles from the cheap liquor store, nobody locks their doors.

In the country, I was told, "'neath the sun and the moon and the big dipper" and not some dim verkakte bulb you'd have to call the super at least once a month to replace, you could walk like a human being down your own flat path to your own front door, past the bright, blinking gazes of furry little woodland things and not the fish-eyed surveillance of the couple in 3C that in four years you've never seen more of than their his-and-hers irises. You could, I was told, and I admit, I believed it and liked the idea of it, you could, in the country, whistle a happy tune down your own flat path to your own front door and, without juggling your grocery bags or hanging your dry cleaning off your lower bridgework so you can free a hand to fish for your keys, simply open it.

There.

See?

In the country, everything is civilized and sensible, carefree and quiet and uncomplicated. Keyless! though not, as it turns out, cowless. I was told, by none other than guess-who, who herself was sold on the *Saturday Evening Post* fairy tale of it all, that in the country, "the country, Dan, think of it!" in the country everything would be all cocktails and convertibles, all chittery chattery happy dappy dipsy doodley dandy and, dammit, we bought it.

No one said boo about the Ed Fences of it all.

No one told us that my son's shrieks would reverberate louder in eight rooms in the middle of nowhere than they did in two and a half rooms in the city.

"Hoo-oo-oo boy!" says Ed, pushing the front door open wide enough so that all my oil heat can escape in one swift swoop. "Some set of lungs that kid has!"

"Won't you come in? All the way?" Myrmy says, polite despite the slight, like an Auto Show hostess who's paid to endure any and every as she coos the finer points of the new DeSoto Firedome. At moments like this, I don't mind that quality in her.

What I do mind is the way Ed's eyes are hugging her curves like a new set of whitewalls. She's my wife and I'm a dog in heat around her under normal circumstance. I put that bun in her oven. But now that her stomach's big as a bakery it doesn't exactly get my yeast rising, pardon the pun, not like it does apparently mister "six under seven!" here. It just ain't kosher. So I peel off my coat and I suck in what's starting to coat my gut and I give Fence a good view of what a former Golden Gloves champ still looks like and I cross my arms, which makes my biceps stand up just that much more and I give him one good heaping helping of "ahem!" and that, Mac, puts an end to that.

All of a sudden he's all innocent, sheepish they call it, foxy I say, like we both don't know that he just ran that stop sign.

Still in the doorway, leaning on the doorknob with what couldn't be more weight than a scarecrow, cowed and scolded but covering, he says to Myrmy, all polite aw-shucks, "sure nice to meet you."

There's something Southern-y in his voice that I didn't notice until now. Probably before marriage and kids and "moderne" house in New England and corporate job and GI-financed schooling and war duty in the Pacific and a bored hooker or two in the big city before shipping out and boot camp before that someplace alien like Florida and kicking it all off for starters a long, long train trip from wherever back home was, a trip on which his heart and his bladder just wouldn't leave him be,

I suspect Ed was probably a good 'ole cracker with an itch or two bigger than his daddy's farm, a polite boy, a mama's boy, whose "sure nice to meet you" would have ended with a "ma'am."

Somewhere along the line, maybe while squirming in the hastily powdered arms of a Flo or a Ruby and shooting too soon though neither seemed to care much, or when he first noticed the shit dribbling down his leg after he shot and killed his first Jap, feeling that soulless feeling like he never felt when trapping possum, or when man met martini and nursed his first fancy hangover, the rube stepping up in class like so many of us did after the storm, Ed stopped with the ma'ams and started with the Macs. At this very moment he's saying neither, and yet, he's saying both. Country shyness and city boldness neither here nor there, there in my doorway with the heat escaping, he's saying neither, but really he's saying both. And in the vapor of that pause between his "sure nice to meet you" and Myrmy's stock, but for her, sincere, "the pleasure is all mine," I'm left racking my brain trying to remember when ma'am turned into Mac for me.

"Hey," Ed says snapping his fingers, "got an idea!" And from there in the open doorway yells out to the autumn air louder than Teddy Roosevelt over the din on San Juan Hill, "Mar-y-y-y? Come on u-u-u-p! Bring the g-i-i-i-rls!"

"I have to lie down," Myrmy says to me under her breath, clearly not up to hostessing on the fly and in her condition who could blame her, "kill me when they arrive."

But they arrive, don't you know, quicker than you can say kaddish.

Mary Fence, as much a little red potato as Ed's a rangy rhubarb stalk, comes whiffling through the tulgy woods burbling "y-o-o-o h-o-o-o! n-e-e-e-ighb-o-o-o-rs! c-a-a-a-ke!" followed by a Whitman Sampler of blonde after blonde after blonde after blonde after blonde after brunette.

"I'm so happy to make your acquaintance," she says, eyes prancing first to Myrmy, then me, then the baby, then the half-unpacked wedding silver and crystal and Book-of-the-Month selections, the sofa piled with hatboxes bearing every store name from one end of Fifth Avenue to the other, the Philco console, the Hitchcock rocker, Hilda in her nurse's whites, ("someone sick?" Mary asks, and re-assessing the baby and Myrmy's belly does a quick two plus two, "oh . . ." and then, sizing up the sterling and hatboxes once more, ". . . my"), all before planting so much as a single potato rhizome into the room, but once she does, brushes right past Ed like he's laundry she's putting off and lifting the lid on a dented tin cake cozy presents Myrmy with her best Betty Crocker pineapple upside-down. "Welcome."

"Girls, hup to!" Ed says, smiling with such pride and love at his distaff half-dozen that I can forgive him the moon, unlaces the youngest from the oldest once the whole litter has mustered the courage to come in, and, setting her down on the braided rug as carefully as you would a kitten, purrs out their names like a contented house tom. "Ellen, Erica, Erin, Edie, Elaine, baby Edwina—meet your new neighbors."

———

For all of Mary's huffing and puffing and spreading and pushing and moaning and milking and barfing and bloating and sagging and stretching across fifty-four, give or take, cumulative months of pregnancy, how is it, Myrmy's been wondering these several hours that the Fences have taken root here, how is it that Mary Fence didn't rate so much as a single letter let alone a full-on namesake?

"We discussed it," Mary tells her, in what sounds to me like forced matter-of-factness while her eyes carefully avoid her husband's side of the sofa, "but Ed feels that names beginning with vowels are so much prettier."

"Mmm . . ." Myrmy mmms in what I know is not at all forced displeasure, while sipping in both Mary's cockeyed explanation and Hilda's latest coffee fiasco. "Does he? So . . . that being the case . . ." she goes on, "A, I, O, and U, I take it, are as low on the totem pole as, say, Emmm for Mar-ee? Emmm for Mer-mee?" And shifting her eyes where Mary's wouldn't tread, "Hmm? Mr. Fffence?"

"Ho-oh, now, you girls!" Ed says, laughing a laugh that won't be the last one Myrmy will never let him live down. Sealing his doom, he settles back on the hatboxes on the sofa, crosses his arms and his legs like the mien were eminent domain, winks at me and says "they forget how hard we work, don't they, buddy boy?"

I don't even have to look. Hilda's rumbly "mm-mm" from over at the playpen tells me that Myrmy's eyes are twin mushroom clouds on that one.

Oh, Fence.

Oh, you poor, poor shmuck.

You've just said the wrong thing in the wrong house in front of the wrong woman and you don't even know it. Even if I tried to explain it to you, you still wouldn't get it, so what's the use, you're going to court all by yourself, who cares what the charges are, if you had any sense, you'd spontaneously combust, buddy boy.

"Mary!" Myrmy says with gusto from out of nowhere. "I don't know how you do it. Six children. All by yourself. With no help. From anyone!"

I didn't see that one coming. God, I love that woman, she's good. Went right past the easy night bombing that would have dropped him quick, right past to the bitter pain of a long, slow winter freeze. With his axis ally in tow, no less.

And out of my mouth come words I can't believe I'm saying. "Ed," I hear myself say, "a little hair of the dog for that coffee?"

"Hmmh," hmmhs Myrmy.

"Hmmh," hmmhs Mary.

I half expect Hilda to "hmmh" in, but as I turn heel toward the kitchen and the cabinet where I think I saw the bottle of Old Grand-Dad's it's Ed's voice that completes the chorus. "Mmmm," he says, savoring rescue, "read my mind, Chief."

"Hmmh," Mary hmmhs once more.

———

Pour a finger or pour a fist, it's all a slap in the face to the wife of a man who drinks. A good look at Mary Fence

and you can see the traces of a girl who got more husband than her wedding toast wished on her. The egg-
beater hairdo. The underbaked complexion. The potato
torso and its loosening hold on posture. These aren't the
charms that brought Fence to her garden gate. Mary's
puffy legs—knees clenched West, ankles crossed East,
in ladylike fashion, in Myrmy fashion—whisper, to me
at least, of a prior privilege about her, like a whiff of My
Sin still on your collar long after neck met neck. Even
the way her pinkie extends, so casually, so automatically,
when she's holding her coffee cup or when she's wiping cake from the chin of one of her brood or when
she's freeing the small cross she wears from the frayed
collar of her cardigan, no matter the chapped skin nor
the chipped nail, speaks as loud to me as her snorted
"hmmh" of a genteel upbringing that never anticipated
being sucker punched by too many quick ones and short
ones and last ones for the road. I doubt that girls like
Mary Fence would ever think to apologize for having
left Goucher or Bryn Mawr or Sweet Briar in their
sophomore or junior or senior years to marry their lusty,
returning, big-dreaming Daves or Bills or Eds. It's not
in their natures, surely not in Mary's from anything I
can tell, to be embarrassed about their abundant propa-

gation, hidden away as so many like her are in wood-
lands such as Eastly, where they can swell and whelp as
anonymously as Gilford's cow. It's not in their natures,
and it's not in my own wife's, I'm proud to say, to shy
away from showing her own fertility publicly, be it on
the mostly male train or at her mostly male office or
any mostlymalewhere she Goddamn well pleases. But
for the Mary Fences of the world, the Mary Fences I'm
guessing this town is filled with, the Mary Fence seated
on my sofa, I wonder if the rewards of motherhood will
always be enough to compensate for all she let go of, and
for the man she let go it all for, the man whose emp-
ties she's sure to be burying, shamed into burying at the
bottom of the trash can, day after day after day, burying
after dinner, not too long after dinner, later tonight not
too long after dinner.

From the looks of it, I'll be tossing that bottle of Old
Grand-Dad's that Ed's shine-to has just about polished
off. I'm sorry, Mary. I'm so very sorry.

Sorry, but then again, not so sorry.

Let's face it, she made her bed same as, say, Hilda
here. And I can't conceive of Hilda being sorry, or ad-
mitting to being sorry that it's other women's offspring
she's paid to love, that she stayed single, that she looks

older, much, much older than the age the agency claims she is, that she can't make coffee to save her life, that even though I'm the one who remembers her name it's Myrmy she defers to, that she's about as warm as an antiseptic, although my son seems to like her so what do I know, that the six little Fence posts have been silently circling her the whole time they've been here, which has been good for us but must be unnerving to her, then again she's as exotic, as glaringly out of place in this house, on this lane, in this town, in her white-white whites as she would be were she Negro, but you don't hear her ruing her lot in life and God help us if she starts because I know what that means, the kid's only two and we've already gone through how many nurses, seven?

—·—

I'd still be flying around the room in a fog bank if Mary hadn't just slapped Ed's knee and said "we should be going," and Ed hadn't pulled it together enough to "huh?" in agreement, and the girls hadn't swarmed to his limbs and yanked at them, chirping "come on, Daddy," and "let's go, Daddy," and "you've got bad breath, Daddy," and "ga, da." Myrmy hoisted herself off the rocker with a "hmmh" and a tsk and taking a long last gander at the girls, hand to her throat, eyes welling, head shaking as if bemused by a miracle, gushed "are they not gorgeous? Oh!"

Because I'm so touched that she's so taken with them, I don't notice Myrmy's hand slump from her throat to just below her breast. So busy am I grinning at my own son who's matching my love with a beam that can break your heart, I don't distinguish the subtle tonal change of her high register "oh" to one of mid-clef surprise. And I'm so village-idiot happy I want to sing hymns that we've done what we've done, trees and all, rake or not, that I don't catch, not like Mary Fence does, the true resonance of the "oh's" sudden plunge to bass clef, pain and anguish keened from primal regions no male will ever know.

Myrmy's doubled over with both hands cradling her abdomen, perched on the edge of the sofa with her skirt hiked high over her knees. The color that should be in her face is washed away, and there's blood form-ing tributaries down her spread legs. She's looking to me for help I don't know how to give, and as I look to Mary, to Ed, to the nurse for the answer I don't know, Myrmy howls. This is a torch song as sacred and sad as Kol Nidre, and I'm scared to learn the words.

"Call the ambulance, Ed," Mary says. "And take the

girls into the other room, will you?" She's all maternal efficiency, fast and fierce and unilaterally female, stroking Myrmy's cheek, holding her hands, hiking her skirt still higher so Hilda can assess, and wordlessly commanding me to usefulness. Take the baby, her eyes are saying. Pick up your son and hold him tight before he knows to cry. The two of them, Mary and Hilda, so practical and competent and calm, more levelheaded than even Eisenhower at the ETO. What men could stand to learn.

"They're on their way," Ed says from the kitchen door, to me, to Mary, soberly and soft. "It won't be long now."

———

They have Myrmy pitched back on the sofa now. Eyes closed. Sobbing with the sound off. I'm at the window with my boy's head on my shoulder, trying not to look over at the thickening blood, trying to resist the urge to cry, to run, to break God's jaw.

Siren's wail, swath of white through the naked trees, pulsars of red and red and red and red and red and the ambulance is turning off the main road, coming into the lane too fast for rubber and gravel to work as one.

At the bottom of the hill, the ambulance skids to a

stop, halfway vanishes behind the great big humpback whale of a rock at the foot of the drive. And just like that, the ambulance is moving again, spitting gravel on its way up to the house, disappearing behind the garage, the siren silenced, but the red and red and red and red and red still throwing faint splashes across the rock and the trees and the yard and the leaves.

And as the attendants sprint with the litter up the flat path to my front door, I see her. Out of the corner of my eye I see her down there. Coming out from behind the rock. Belly heavy, swollen low. Looking up at me with good-bye in her sloe, sad eyes.

The cow.

THREE

And the years go by.

$\mathcal{S}$TART WITH THE FOUNDATION.

Sweep the pad in clean arcs across the forehead first, encouraging the liquid to exalt in the sense of its own purpose. Silken coolness slipping from the eyebrows upwards, shimmer of new adventure as tiny pavé pools catch the light, slink it, sheen ever higher, across the taut expanse of forehead where lines have yet to taunt. Phosphorescence gilds pore upon pore as the pad brushes higher still, becoming careful pat sweeps skimming along the hairline's twill horizon. Pat sweeps of pad and lotion up and over the summit of high-cresting cheekbone, encoring across the divide, double back and up and over and dovetail down the fine bone of strong nose, straight and unencumbered by bump or precipice. Mouth and jaw slacken to allow firm comma sweeps in the hollow behind each nostril, above the lip a jaunty swath, dibdab to the bevel of nose tip. Then, mouth and jaw returned to grace, lips full, mouth lineless, as the finishing sweep of silken coolness welcomes the chin to the party.

Oh, the poetry of skin at thirty-eight.

—·—

Give me the quiet of an early morning, the quiet darkness of an early morning, in an oasis of light at my makeup mirror. I will give you my heart if you just give me this hour.

Give me Dan in the kitchen and the children asleep, and Nettie not yet shlumping about to debate chicken over lamb for dinner. Let me sit here, freshly bathed, incandescent in my bra and girdle and slip and stockings, on a roman bench upholstered in white shantung. This is my throne and the mirror my public and the shadows and rouges and polishes and pencils the jewels of my kingdom and do not disturb my reign.

Give me the alchemy that packaging promises, that brings out my eyes and raises my cheeks and softens my nose and lushens my lips. Leave me to trace a slim finger lingeringly down the clean line of my throat and admire its cascade to smooth clavicle, then flutter last night's manicure out for a second opinion. Yes, the PinkRed was a good choice; it takes the focus off my fingers where the knuckles are just beginning to ripple.

I don't want to hear that the oilman comes today and that he'll need a check, or that yesterday's milk delivery froze in the box and exploded bluewhite. It's 5 a.m. and you may have me at 6, but from now until then I'm strictly single-o.

———

The hazel of my eyes, Martin once said over peppermint fizzes, reminded him of heirloom damask, and although I'm not sorry I threw him over for his effeteness, I always did appreciate his eye for fabrics. Lowell had a thing for my delicate ears and my unhooked nose as he indelicately put it, and because he, too, had an unhooked nose felt that any children we might have would be twice as likely to not look homely or rabbinical. He had a point. But after his family flew me to Florida and I baked in that sun and my nose and every other inch of my skin freckled for all eternity, irrational as it may be, I never forgave him, nice as his sisters were to me, but, oy, that mother . . .

Sacrosanct are my lips. Be they RedRed or RustRed or RubyRed or RocketRed, LuxeRed or RascalRed or BetterRedThanDeadRed. Sealed and relaxed or open for the taking, they're my Scylla and Charybdis and they sing my siren's song.

What the hell. Go with the metaphor:

Red sky at morning, sailor take warning. Red sky at night, sailor take fright. Woe to the mariner who's smug in my waters. I may glisten and undulate in my makeup and tailored wardrobe, but my depths are rife with uncharted reefs and the course to my heart takes careful navigation.

Howard thought he knew my coordinates.

"You're not like other women," he said. Tall, sleek Howard, the Jew who took me sailing. Whose mind could do somersaults. Howard who could play tennis, and speak French, and boasted "we both know I'm the man for you."

Howard, for whom success, we also both were certain, was as inevitable as death, made a grave assumption that his love would validate me more than any career. "I have a future," he said. "I'll worry for the both of us," he said. "Relax," he said. "Tear up your résumé and marry me," he said and said. And then had the gall to say it

again, a final time, in that ultimatum he had that secretary of mine take down that day I lunched out for
a change. "Marry me," her note read, "or I'm marrying
another. It's the last time I'll ask you. Call me by 1, or
I'm marrying another." She was filing her nails when I
sailed in at 2.

And then, there was Dan.

Roommate to a Friday-night fix-up. Picked up the
phone when I called to confirm, liked what he heard and
flirted from the get-go. "I guess we should meet if we're
gonna get married," he said. "I'll tell what's-his-name ya
busy t'morra night."

That Boston burn to his deep voice, tough-guy
smooth and who did he think he was? Nine months
since Howard's missed phone call and now the wrong
party and it just felt right.

What a perfect cup of coffee he seemed. Not too
weak to ridicule my independence, nor strong enough to
fear it. Sure, it was a jolt. Ten years older with a résumé
full of roughhousing not like any Jewish boy, Jewish
man I ever met. Minor League baseball, and boxing of
all things, hat-check concessions with his father in Joe
Kennedy's untalked-about speakeasies, cargo boats to
South America, then the army before we needed it and

still in when we met long after, and an ex-wife who, fool that she was, or maybe wasn't, couldn't see the forest for the trees. He was so rough around the edges, brute built, but educated, and articulate even in a daffy kind of way. Liked the paint-by-numbers discipline of the hup-to life, as he called it, yet had a makeshift darkroom in his bathroom where he'd singe his hands night after night experimenting with color.

He leapt hard for me, like he was still in the ring and wanted that title bad, and before I knew it I was in his bed, twenty-six and still living in my mother's house and lying to her so I could return to him for another twelve rounds before I even brought him home to meet her, to meet my grandmother.

And then when I did and he wore that leather bomber jacket like he was just a guy, and I was just a gal, and they were just my folks, and it was just a Sunday afternoon . . .

"How could you?" I said afterwards, spitting out the words, MadRed and so ashamed of his filling-station bearing, and ashamed of myself for the obvious rebellion that falling for him was, jerking my arm away from him as he tried to clasp my elbow on the way down the stoop, my mother coiling into a smile at that, I'm sure, from a fold in the parlor shades.

"You made up your own God-damned mind," he said to my back, and I could tell from his voice his teeth had no intention of unclenching. "It was your call, all the way." When I didn't hear the thudclick of his boots behind me any longer, I slowed to quiet the clapclick of my heels, and then stopped altogether. It wasn't long before he started to walk again, and talk again. "If it's Howard you all want," he went on, "ya shit out of luck."

Was it then that I realized we were in the same boat, or did the revelation come later on, afloat on Malaschalk's couch? I'm not sure. Memory is such a sloppy librarian. Either way, it dawned on me clear as sitting at this mirror now that for all my sex-defying independence, I didn't have the strength to break my mother's mooring ropes; and for all his hup-to anchoring, he harbored a yearning for riptides. And that the two seeming opposites weren't all that polar. And that like a face full of incongruities, we, too, could flow as one.

And maybe I would bring out his best.

And maybe he would lance my worst.

And maybe together we would balance each other out.

And lift each other up.

And buoy each other along.

And have a family.

And have a life.

And look, on the surface at least, like other people.

So instead of marching him to the subway that night and snubbing him off my radar for good, I ricocheted with him from Brooklyn back into the city, and the next day, walling my ears to my mother's cries and my grandmother's fake fainting gasps, moved in with him. And for the next four years made his bed ours and his closets mine. And not a moment too late for those wailing women came the red-letter day, eight years ago today, that I wore ivory satin and married him, married him, married him.

———

Eight years ago today. The Ides of March.

And not a single person said beware the cost of a double life. Worker and wife, careerist and companion. And mother.

Eight years and four jobs and five pregnancies and meetings and train schedules and formula and diapers and deadlines and clients and mortgage and croup and a revolving door of baby nurses until Nettie, thank God, and Dan stagnating in that civilian job I convinced him to take when the army wanted him back for Korea of all things, they got Elvis, they didn't need Dan, a man of his age, for crying out loud, and after what they did to him in that hospital upstate . . .

Mrs. Kennedy, eat your heart out. You're not the only one who can carry off the box cut of this wool suit without looking like the extra roominess is necessary. Five pregnancies for me and not much fuller considering, how do you like that? You and I, Mrs. JFK, twin sheaves of goldenrod bouclé in our full-length mirrors at dawn's early light. Do you even care that I paid for mine while yours was paid for by the man you married? I do.

The choice would have been nice: to know I could pay my own way, yet not have to.

But you, lucky girl, society shikse with your glad rags and golden guy, what do you know about real life? You don't have to leave the house too early to kiss the children awake so that you can find a parking space in the same time zone, nor crowd onto the station platform without losing your hat to all those open newspapers, nor second-guess the headlight and horn of the train rounding the bend—is it the express or is it ours?— and then fall into a seat next to your husband who's already fallen asleep before you've had a chance to find your lighter, the pearl-handled one he gave you as an anniversary gift last year. And as you stare out the window at the parade of trees and factories and houses and cars that start to come and go, come and go as the train picks up speed do you suddenly see your reflection blast back at you like the tunnel you've just whooshed into, only to see the fatigue in your face that you didn't see earlier in that more charitable light. There in the low glow as the train chugs and jostles you wonder how that form chugging and jostling in its sleep on the seat beside you thickened and slackened so soon, so much, and even though it's your husband, you look around to see who's noticing and you elbow it to stop it from snoring, from embarrassing you with its snoring. All those other suits surrounding you in the train car, not a pinstripe out of place, crisp as their morning commute. You follow the thread through, wondering why none of them seem to crease with the weight of their days, rumple under the burdens of job-wife-kids the way your man has, the way you have not, and that's when you buttonhole the answer that suits: he's done you a favor. He's taken your grief and borne its girth for you, let it get the better of him for you, even when it was you and I, Jacqueline, you and I who gave birth to all of those dead babies.

Eight years and four jobs and five pregnancies and the miscarriage not long after we moved up there, and then, that sweet thing a year after that with the hole in his heart who never lived long enough for us to give him a name and I can still fit in my wedding dress, but Dan's suit wouldn't recognize him now. Five boys and three survived, and so fragile and little and alive I'm afraid to touch them. The nurses weren't, and Nettie isn't, and Dan's not, so why am I?

———

Thank God for the thrum of Grand Central where you come alive, I come alive, she comes alive. The she who protects her lipstick by offering her husband a good-bye cheek at the Vanderbilt entrance, who clicks and tinkles her way on a ribbon of fragrance up Madison to her world away from home. Such happy purpose, such competence, funny and sparkly and quick-as-all-get-out, top of her game her associates all marvel, how does she do it with children to boot?

The how is a why, and the why is because.

Here in my element I know who I am. Carbon and oxygen and Revlon and Bergdorf's and adjectives and verbs and "did you read . . ." and "have you seen . . ." and "where did you find . . ." and "you won't believe. . . ." Palpitating at my typewriter I'm no ordinary Gal Monday-through-Friday, I'm the one from Brooklyn who's all Harper's

Bazaar, earning as much as the wing tips and neckties and more than her own husband, not that they need know. I'm the one they pay to work from home when my pregnancies become too obvious for their comfort, paid to stay out of sight to stitch pitches for laundry soap and breakfast cereal to women in the same state of disgrace, defining for them who "she" is and what "she" buys and where "she" shops and when. Who cares if they don't invite me to their restricted country clubs. As long as they keep raising my shekels, let them pay their own dues. I'm the one they swear leads a double life as adroitly as a double agent. Click on the desk lamp she's Madison Avenue. Click it off and she's honey and Mommy. They think me Jupiter running rings around Saturn, and from nine to five I'm inclined to agree.

But get me back to the Vanderbilt entrance and the clock and the Concourse and the 5:25 and Dan rumpled and sweating and the bar car and the track's shrill squeal and the windows mercifully steamed over so I can't see Pluto fade into the distance nor the vein in my forehead start to jump, get me back to the station as dusk dies and into the car and onto the road in a slow-moving stream of taillights, and back to the house in the woods and the children, fed and washed and a story and kiss away from bed, and Nettie looking more blue than black in the kitchen's fluorescent light with that one-eyed half-smile of hers at me that says "Mizzuz, you ain't gonna believe what that lil one done . . ." get me back to all that and I have to ask myself: do I live in the country and commute to the city or is that table turned?

Then I remember there's my new satin brocade and the tuxedo I bought for Dan and the anniversary dinner in our honor at Gene and Mae Swoon's tonight. Highballs and deviled eggs and the men from the train I've befriended for us and the wives I'm getting to know and wanting to like and struggling to keep pace with. Me with my career and my smart clothes and my housekeeper—you will be baking cupcakes for the nursery-school picnic, won't you? All those willing Penelopes, Band-Aiding and sponge-bathing and crown-roasting and weaving and waiting for their husbands to come home from their odysseys beyond the tracks. And me, such a washout with a needle and thread. But at least I try to hold my own, unlike Dan who unlike himself will no more swoon than he will swagger these days among those hens and Howards.

———

Late tonight with the moon knifing through curtain and valance I'll settle my hips under his weight the way I've learned to do and watch our shadows writhe.

"Happy anniversary," I'll say to him.

"Are you happy?" he's asked me more than once.

"Yes, aren't you?" I shouldn't inquire, but could.

"I love you, you know," I may have heard him say.

"I love you, too," one or both of us hasn't said from time to time.

"I love you, too," I hope I say tonight.

"Are you coming, or what?" I hear him saying to the mirror out in the hall. "You don't want to miss the train."

FOUR

Ties.

Lᴇᴛ's ɢᴇᴛ ᴏɴᴇ ᴛʜɪɴɢ sᴛʀᴀɪɢʜᴛ ʀɪɢʜᴛ ʜᴇʀᴇ, right now.

I did not turn west instead of east on Route 5A, bypassing the right turn with that nice easy repose to it and opting instead to fishtail into that sharp left just beyond the rotary, contrary to what a certain someone in the car thinks, because I wanted to "head (us) in the wrong direction," "just to make (her) crazy," because it's "so like (me) to go out of (my) way to add an extra two hours to the trip," much as it may seem that "(I) do this all the time," like (she) should talk.

No, I did not turn west instead of east on Route 5A just for the hell of it.

I turned west instead of east on Route 5A because it

was 96 degrees and 200 percent humidity and something rotting in the cooler in the back smelled worse than a pulp mill and I was sick of playing "Spelling Bee."

I was sick of playing "Spelling Bee," and the boys were sick of playing "Spelling Bee," and Nettie has trouble enough dialing the phone so lucky (her) she was left out of playing "Spelling Bee," and the only one who was enjoying playing "Spelling Bee" was guess who, and if she went from giving Charlie a word like "cup" to giving me a word like "solipsism" one more time, folding her arms and giving me her "I dare you" look one more time, I was gonna slam on the brakes and kick open the door and unstick my thighs from the plastic seat and march to the back and tear off the tailgate and chuck out every last damn piece of luggage and the cooler and the beach chairs and the sand toys until I found one of the boys' inflatable rafts, and I was gonna take one of those rafts and inflate it and then shove it over Miss Fuckin' Wagnall's face and make her spell "asphyxiate."

———·———

You're driving along the Interstate on a hot July day, following the route that the motor club marked in red on your map for you, driving along in your four-year-old

station wagon with its dented rocker panel and its broken horn, heading off with your wife and your three boys
and the housekeeper and more crap than got dumped
in the Berlin air drop to spend two weeks on the neck
of Rhode Island in a town called Squishapogue, which
even the motor club had trouble locating on the map in
order to circle it in blue, on your way to a rented cabin
that you've never seen and aren't even sure has indoor
plumbing; detouring onto the surface road where the
Interstate comes to its abrupt end with no more warning
than a couple of flame pots and a sign reading "Highway
Completion Date:" with the date missing; thinking
all the while that the unfinished highway has to be a
smoother ride than the surface road's rutted macadam
that can't be a holiday for your axles; driving along, heat
blasting like the sun was tied to your roof rack, bug guts
splattered all over your windshield, your ten-year-old
kicking the back of your seat because he has to wee-
wee and wants you to stop "now!" and your six-year-old
kicking the back of your seat just because the ten-year-
old is kicking it "so (he) can, too!" and you're not even
sure if your four-year-old is still breathing because his
face is buried somewhere behind the housekeeper's left
tit and that one tit alone is the size of Montana, and

the housekeeper keeps dabbing at the folds of her neck with a hankie so sopped it can't possibly absorb one more drop of sweat, and your wife's up front with you on the other side of your camera bag and her pocketbook and her knitting box and sweaters for the boys "in case it gets cold," fanning herself with the motor club's map while spelling out "guillotine" with all the self-satisfaction of a state trooper who'd goose step sooner than he'd let you off with a speeding warning; you're driving, you're sweating, you're spelling "recalcitrant," your head is pounding as much as the back of your seat, and you know somewhere in the back of your mind you're supposed to be thinking to yourself "ah, this is the life," and yet, for some crazy reason, hard as it may be to believe, you just can't quite tune your dial to that station.

———·———

I sell neckties for a living. Three weeks of every month I sit at a desk that's missing two of its seven drawers and staple together fabric sample batches, six six-inch-square fabric swatches per sample batch, each batch bound by a folded band of white cardboard one-half-inch wide.

One week out of every month I travel to cities such as Akron, Fort Wayne, and/or Tupelo, and I meet with the buyers of regional department stores and the finer regional men's haberdasheries. I fan out my sample batches on desks missing only one of the seven drawers and I look straight as I can into the wandering eyes of the Mel's and the Gus's and the occasional Miss Burns's, and I say with great enthusiasm: "This season, on our Silver Standard line, the silver stripe is wider than the navy/burgundy/green/gold/brown/powder blue stripes. Our Triple Diamond line features an exciting change, too. The centered clocking now boasts overlapping diamonds of different colors. So you could have clocking in navy, burgundy and green, say, against a field of gold, brown, or powder blue. And your more adventurous customers will appreciate our Apollo Line, which is the updated version of our Mercury Line, on which the rocket ships now come in a choice of navy/burgundy/green/gold/brown/powder blue against a celestial galaxy of navy/burgundy/green/gold/brown/powder blue."

I then fix on what I think is their one good eye and I ask the Mel's, Gus's, and/or occasional Miss Burns's how many neckties they would like to order. When they tell me, I write down the order on a form that comes in triplicate—white copy for them, yellow copy for inventory & shipping back at the office, and pink copy for me.

In the army, every form was in triplicate, too, whether it was a requisition for toilet paper or a bill of lading for torpedoes, so I'm an old hand at forms in triplicate and this fact may very well have been the reason I was hired. I then return to home and resume stapling sample batches for the next month's trip to places like Spokane, Keokuk, and/or Kankakee. For this I am paid a base salary plus commission, commission being based on the total number of sales on my total amount of pink copies, minus expenses, sick leave, and the estimated average of re-order sales that would have come in had I visited my accounts or not. I get two weeks' vacation per year.

The one week per month that I'm on the road to places like Fresno, Sandusky and/or Enid, I resist any and all temptations to suddenly pull an about-face and toodle over someplace madcap like Vicksburg, Smyrna and/or Orono. I do what I'm paid to do. I do what my wife asked me to do before the ink on our marriage certificate had time to run, which was apply myself to a civilian job and leave the service for good. But, because businesses wanted young men they could train from the ground up, and because I was much older than most of the returning vets, not just from one war but two, I took one of the few jobs that would have me, and have me it does.

I don't veer, I don't detour, I don't toodle, I don't fish-tail. There is nothing that I do in my job that I do just for the hell of it.

So if, behind the wheel of my '59 Rambler station wagon, with its little fins over the taillights that are meant to make me feel aerodynamic, if I should suddenly opt for the unexpected in the middle of spelling "supere-rogatory" and turn where I'm not supposed to turn, "you were supposed to turn!" and head us in the direction of Quamasmegmalalohogue instead of Squishapogue, "pu-erile" and "duplicitous" and "misogamistic" as some may see it, I think I've earned the right and, agree or not, someone had better just keep her yap snapped.

"This is a fine how do you do."

So much for yap-snapping.

"I have to wee-wee!"

"OK, there's a gas station up ahead."

"What kind is it?"

"It's an Esso, all right?"

"No!"

"What do you mean, no?"

"It has to be Sinclair! It has to have the dinosaur!"

"Well, it's an Esso, Adam, so . . . so . . ."

"You'll wee-wee where we tell you to wee-wee."

Listen to her. All of a sudden she's Douglas MacArthur.

"I have to pie."

"You can do that at the Esso."

"Hurry up, it's coming."

"All right, Charlie . . ."

"We're supposed to pick up the keys by three."

"We'll get there."

"We'll get there?"

"You wanna drive?"

"In this traffic?"

"I have to pie, Daddy. Hurryuphurryuphurryup!"

"Shut up, Charlie, I have to wee-wee and I get to go first, don't I get to go first, Daddy?"

"Hang on, we're almost there, you'll both get to go."

"I bet there was a gas station closer if you had turned where you were supposed to turn."

"Nettie, does Josh need to go?"

"Hmmm?"

"Josh. Does he need to go?"

"Not anymore."

"Ew!"

"Ew, gross!"

"Ew, gross doubled!"

"Why didn't you turn?"
"Who wants to get hit?"
Silence.
Sniffle.
Esso.

———

Give Nettie a recipe to follow, or a postcard to read, or written instructions of any kind, and you may as well have asked her her weight. She'll hmph and squint off into the vague distance like she just heard the noon whistle, or better, was following whatever it was you gave her to read as it kamikazeed off with the evening breeze. She'll fish in her pocket for her tin of snuff, unscrew its lid as carefully as if it were a bomb fuse, take a pinch no bigger than the bumpy pads of her plump fingers, and tuck and tamp it wherever her teeth aren't. For some reason I'll never understand, she'll turn her head just enough so you can see the small thickets of white hairs behind her ears that want out from under her chestnut wig. And only then will she speak, saying, to no one in particular, me particularly, "I have work to do." And to drive home that her words are the last, she'll spit out a fleck of snuff.

Pthew.

I often forget that Nettie can't read. Whether she never learned, or never had much occasion to need to, I don't know and she won't say. The agency never mentioned it to Myrmy when they phoned to tell her they'd found "the perfect girl" for their "favorite repeat client."

At the time, Myrmy didn't care if she was perfect, or even if she was a girl. What turned out to be the last of the parade of professional baby nurses hotfooted it only a few months after Josh was born, clunked open her plaid valise, packed her two starched whites and her nurse's orthopedics and her hot water bottle and her Bible and planted herself by the front door until I volunteered to drive her to the station. Packed and planted herself there posture-perfect one Sunday night only minutes after taking a moocher's snort from her tincture of ammonium bottle upon hearing Myrmy announce her plan to stay at home indefinitely:

"I'm not retiring," Myrmy said. "I'm just going to be Mommy for a while. And we'll see how it goes."

And Glenda, or Mona, or Miss Hale, or Nurse Breen, or whatever her name was, must have seen all too clear how it would go, I guess, having underfoot twenty-six hours a day, nine days a week, a six-year-old, a three-year-old, an infant and "your Missus," as she referred to my wife to me, because in her germ-free nurse's logic she concluded:

"You see. I quit."

Quite soon, Myrmy saw.

Three changed diapers, an eyeful of Desitin, and an admonishing earful of "you'd turn red, too, if you were bathed in water that hot!" from the pediatrician who took her emergency calls soon. The next afternoon, Nettie hmphed and pthewed down the steps of the 3:07, onto the platform and into our lives.

———

When you have a wife who works, who works and makes a lot of money, who works and makes a lot more money than you, you're not the head of the household, Torah, Talmud, Frank and Deano and Sammy and dick and balls notwithstanding, not by a long shot. Financial decisions aren't made by you and seconded or scoffed at by your missus; it's you who does the seconding and scoffing, seconding more and scoffing less as the years advance. So we have a fine enough house in a good enough town. One car, not two, not sporty, not new. A new living room, however, for entertaining, and a new master bedroom built mostly for the new bathroom and the new walk-in closet filled with the ever-expanding wardrobe of new dresses and new hats and new shoes and new pocketbooks, and the odd new suit here or there in ever-expanding waist and trunk size, and neckties. We have bank accounts started in all three children's names for the educations that all the Winnie the Pooh-ing and Dr. Seuss-ing are priming their brains for. We haven't gone to Disneyland and probably never will, but we've driven to the Florida sun and felt the spray off Niagara Falls. And, not because we're grand or ring-a-ding-dingy or genetically predisposed to it, we have a housekeeper, not a maid, a housekeeper. Though call her a heartkeeper and you're more on the money.

When you have a wife who works, making good money or not, somebody has to take care of your children. When one of them is pretending he's a high-wire act, tiptoe teetering head down on the railroad ties that line your front path and thwumps forehead first into an oak, somebody has to be there. When the dog is giving birth to her first litter of purebreds, giving birth on the playroom couch in front of your boys, keeping them as entertained as an episode of *Bonanza* up until she rolls over and eats the runt and makes them shriek like it was

Chiller Theater, somebody has to be there. Somebody has to be there to feed them breakfast after we've left for the train and dinner before we've returned on it. Somebody has to be there for the daytime thunderstorms and the garter snakes and the clay handprints and the chicken pox and the Adam-took-my-trucks and Charlie-hit-mes and when's-Mommy-coming-homes. Somebody has to be there for their childhood and who cares if she can read, can she love?

Clean dishes, clean laundry, clean toilets, clean floors: they get done. If and when there's time, in between kisses on foreheads and knee hugs and "who's my great big boys" and pthews, they get done. It's a fringe benefit we're grateful for, certainly, but neither of us, Myrmy especially, surprisingly, more than me, neither of us would ever dare chase after Nettie with a white glove. She has our children's hearts in the palm of her hand.

Although we don't talk in front of her about who brings home what bacon, Nettie knows who butters her bread and it has nothing to do with dough. She sees Myrmy dressed to the nines at 6 a.m., breathes in deep the perfume of the day and hmphs her approving hmph. She coordinates all the parcels that arrive by UPS from Bonwit Teller and Lord & Taylor and Saks, and all the parcels that get returned by UPS to Bonwit Teller and Lord & Taylor and Saks, and never does she ever give me her disapproving hmph even though we all know who doesn't pay for the stuff that comes and goes back. Polite as she is to me, polite and folksy and warm, unless I give her something to read and it's squint-screw-pinch-tamp-turn-speak-pthew, in her eyes, behind her smudged glasses, I'm not the head of the house, for one reason and one reason only.

I'm a man.

Colored or not, wealthy or not, a much better cook than her or not, I'm a man. End of story.

I'm just a man, but Myrmy is a Woman.

And more than that, she's a Woman who's gone through the Pain of Labor.

A Woman who's gone through the Pain of Labor who Works.

And I'll be God-damned if the Two of Them aren't on the Same Page.

We could be in the car, or at the dinner table, or triangulated in the hall from the kitchen to the back bedrooms, and I'll see the two of them share "the look," which means the Uri Geller mind-reading act is about to begin and it's say-good night-Gracie time for me.

Picture a cobweb stuck to a soffit, indistinguishable from the veins in the knotty pine paneling, call it a man, and it's my eyes that see:

Predictably: Myrmy, out of makeup and in her robe, at the table after Friday dinner, the day's mail and the night's Sanka in front of her offering little in the way of kicks or comfort.

Fortunately: Nettie, in the kitchen, humped over the sink, adjusting her glasses with a handful of soapsuds.

Inexplicably: out of nowhere: tandem head turns. 45 degrees to the right meets 45 degrees to the left.

Inevitably: "the look," as it passes through the pass-through, from Myrmy's almond eyes in the dining room to Nettie's filberts in the kitchen.

Incomprehensibly: Nettie's one-eyed smile of understanding.

Resourcefully: she dries her wet hands on her apron, sledding them down from her Blue Ridge Mountains to her Hip-alayas.

Matter-of-factly: she asks:

"Aaasprin? Or Milltowwwn?"

And wearily: Myrmy answers:

"One of each."

Maddeningly: Myrmy's relief at being understood,

her shoulders releasing their choke hold from her neck, the smallest smile giving her cheeks a reason for living.

Finally: look up, up to the ceiling, up to the soffit and the cobweb that's me. Look into my eyes, brown, blood-shot, almond-shaped, "incredulous." I'm spinning you nothing extraordinary. Just my web, and welcome to it.

———

My web, Myrmy's web, Nettie's web. All of us spinning our own tidy cradles out of fine silk thread, hoping with every fiber we're the catchalls and not the caught, yet knowing full well we're all just a broom stroke away from nine kinds of oblivion.

Down the Atlantic a sweep, down far deep in North Carolina, off the main road and not on any map, Nettie's antique husband, Winter, goes web for web with his ab-sent wife. Fueled on Old Crow and Jim Crow, he's hell for broke down the middle of the town road on his thirdhand John Deere. Not no license nor no registra-tion can keep him from plowing straight into trouble when the mood strikes, liquored by night and, lately, by day. When the trouble comes, and it comes seasonally, it seems, even though he knows better, when it comes and the local law stops him in his tracks and locks him away, as much for his color as his crime, it's not their grown daughter who lives an hour west who gets the call, nor Winter's brother in the next county, the one they didn't hang, nor Nettie's sister on the rag end of town, it's Nettie they wire to set his bail and haul his used-up ass home. Nettie, the nigger's wife who works up North, the washerwoman, the mammy, the maid whose tender care of other people's children paid for that used tractor, and the barn it rusts in, and the house it leans toward, and the truck farm it lists on.

It's Nettie who pthews bullets as Myrmy reads her the wire. Nettie who dries shame tears with the bunched edge of her apron as Myrmy strokes her shoulder, and gives her an envelope full of cash, and gives her a round-trip train ticket, and gives her "the look" that's a look beyond all looks. Nettie who takes the look and swallows it without chewing and trades her apron for her good traveling coat, one of Myrmy's better castoffs, and sets South to spring Winter.

Adding my two cents, I stock her with a half-dozen tins of her favorite snuff, the snuff the tobacco store by the station stocks for me for her, thinking maybe, maybe, after handing over the bail money and scratching her X on the release forms; after huffing dust on the ride back to their farm in the bed of the neighbor's pickup; after strong-arming open the barn door to make sure that the tractor was returned; after wiping her glasses clean to inspect their four-room house as much for mess as for possible signs of another woman's touch; after burning his dinner on purpose and finally, finally torching him with her anger, only to bite her tongue when the mesh of ropy fingers he buries his face in tugs her back to a teenage night, and his hand on her cheek, and the dream he spun that wasn't going to be this; maybe then, maybe then she'll give him half, or two, or one of the tins of snuff at least, in forgiveness and compassion, from a wife he rarely gets to see, for a life he has limited say in. Give it to him in forgiveness and compassion, and sympathy by proxy, sympathy from a white man up North who doesn't know much and won't pretend he does. I sell neckties and Winter knows nooses and God strike me down if I ever knot the two.

I crushed the glass and married the comet. I left the service to staple the samples and travel to Bismarck and sell Silver Stripes. I fathered the boys. And booked the movers. And chose the car. And ordered the snuff. And turned left when I felt like it. I let my legs scab and my gut go without a fight.

I'm the one who stood in front of the X-ray machine
in that hospital upstate. Stripped my uniform down to
my shorts and stood full five-nine, no T-shirt and no
lead pad, and no waiver signed in triplicate.

I'm the one who followed their orders.

And hupped to the look.

Who didn't ask: why?

Or say: no.

FIVE

What is this thing called love?

---

o.

That's all you had to say.

To the Clerk. The Staff Sergeant. Your Commanding Officer, and I use the term loosely. To the Medic, or the Technician, or the Doctor he should lose his license, to all of them:

No.

Defiantly.

Defensibly.

Definitively.

In triplicate.

No.

Why is it that certain men cannot say no?

"And when you should have taken them to court,

when you had the chance, you didn't, you wouldn't," I've said to him so many times it's as routine and pointless as asking why the President had to go to Dallas.

"Are you finished?" he'll say to me.

And, knowing that it's useless, I stop talking. I don't give him the no that he wouldn't give them, I'm finished, but I'm not finished, and he knows that I'm not finished. I'm just finished for now.

And then the boys do something, or the dogs do something, or Heidi does something, inches up to the door with an admonishing finger to her lips in a way that Nettie would have never dared, or the phone rings, or the light turns green, or nothing at all happens, which is worse than anything, and that's that.

And on we go.

———

Cole Porter never wrote songs for couples like us. Couples who have children and dogs and freezers rusting in the garage and problems that can't be solved la-dee-da, like it was just one of those things.

Couples who always have champagne at the ready, he wrote for. Couples who are just falling in love, whether it's been for sale or not, riding its gossamer wings night and day, getting their kicks out of nothing but each other, (unless it's too darn hot), so in love, he wrote for. Well, Miss Otis here regrets to inform that something's been done to me, to all of us, that hardly goes. Anything but.

When my custom-tailored vet took me out for something wet, and my vet began to pet and I cried "hooray . . ." little did I anticipate that in short order he'd stand in front of an X-ray machine in an army hospital in upstate New York, lead pad folded away in a cupboard or maybe draped in the corner on a table in full view, stand there dark and virile as John Garfield, stripped to his Skivvies, not a thing covering his chest, that chest that was made for medals, stand there stiff and proud and strong as if about to salute, as they methodically engaged their machine, juiced it carefully, according to the manual, according to orders, for their experiment, for their research, adjusted a lever here and turned a dial there and shot him.

Orders from the top brass.

Personnel selected at random.

Compliance in writing deemed unnecessary at this time.

Phase II research on effects of radiation from, or indirectly related to, atomic exposure.

All information classified per directive of the Department of Defense.

All, except what he'd gotten under his skin when they burned out his thyroid. That bit of information they couldn't keep classified. No. That leaked. Inside him.

Just as we were beginning our own version of the Beguine.

Little things at first. Light-headedness if he leapt too fast out of bed in the morning, eager to take on the day. Shaving nicks that took longer than usual to clot, regardless of tissue paper or styptic pencil. Fatigue that bore no correlation to physical exertion. They came about so subtle and random the symptoms we didn't even make a connection. We laughed that he was just getting older. The world was ours for the taking, GE and GM and CBS said so, but maybe he'd need to take it just a little bit slower. "Are you really up for all of this," I said to him early on when pregnant with Adam, my hand at home on his chest, red nails playing hide-and-seek under all that dark hair. "You betcha," he said back, the words firm and sure, rumbling through his chest, through my fingertips, right into my DNA.

Cells are born and cells divide and somewhere in their nuclei rumors started spreading. Bits and pieces found their way through trapdoors down back alleys, climbed in windows and jimmied locks. All those spoiled hormones, mutant and renegade, sneaking like the Rosenbergs with their dirty information from his thyroid hither and yon, forcing open sewer lids of skin on his arms and legs, dots that grew to patches, tossed aside so that all that subterfuge could bubble up for all to see.

By the time the two dead babies were behind us and Charlie was born, light-headedness had become dizzy spells, extended stays in rooms without air.

"It's not nothing," I'd say to him. "There's a reason this is happening. Something's wrong. Will you go to the doctor already?"

But he wouldn't say yes. Made excuses. Started to eat, and overdo it.

With Josh's birth the sleeping began. Sudden fits of it. Early evening. Late morning. Mid-afternoon. Unexpected as door-to-door salesmen, and as aggressive as the best of them. No need to call us, they made it clear. We'll call on you. In front of *Ed Sullivan* at first. Then at his desk. Then behind the wheel.

Driving up the main road, where the hill is a curve over a culvert for a stream, Adam wasn't fast enough to stop what was happening, didn't look up soon enough from the book in his lap to realize that Daddy had fallen asleep, all he could take in was the guardrail getting closer and the stream flowing darker and Daddy not reacting and the car horns and the rail and the head-light breaking and the bumper and the bolts and the tire going off and the hood over the water, Mommy, his side of the car through the rail and off the road and hanging over the water and his book at his feet and his shoulder slugged and Daddy's eyes wide open now, really wide open, and breathing hard, and his arm across Adam's chest holding him back so hard it was hard to cry, pro-tecting him like he would have done if he wasn't out, if he'd been awake, if he'd only said no.

What is this thing called? Love?

———

The little that you do know beyond the "no" that never came—the burned-out thyroid, the "remote possibility" of complications, the advice from the very perpetrators of the crime to "go on about your life, Captain"—what are you supposed to do with it?

You can only do so much for a man who won't do for himself. Dress it up and do it for him by doing it for yourself, for your children, keeping him included, yes, of course, but only as one of many and not head of you all. So stepping up for the two of you, for all five of you, it's you—Peck & Pecking your way up and down all those corridors. Working staff and moonlighting freelance, taking jobs for the money and not the cachet, and certainly not for the thrill of divining that thing inside of you that you know is there waiting to be tapped. You keep your figure educated at Slenderella in the new math of curves-times-calories, not for him, but because your tailored hips get you in office doors as much as any padded letters of recommendation, as much as your smarts and, let's face it, you're not getting any less Jewish. Though smart girl that you think you are, there's no dieting away what's hiding in wait for all of you, for him above all, no willing your life into a perfect size 4. You have no more control over it than you do over next year's hemlines.

Fashions change, but your fears are four-season. In the autumn, you can them in Ball jars of marmalade and apple chutney, spoon in the sugar and bring them to a boil, then warm the paraffin and seal them tight. You tamp your concerns into the earth with every tulip bulb and daffodil and crocus and gladiola, and here and there a hyacinth, so what if they don't last long. Winter snows a fine throw for wrapping yourself in milestones: birth-day parties one after another for the children, white cakes with chocolate icing and aren't you something with that pastry tube spelling out their names in blue. Follow the patterns from Simplicity, (ha! whom are they kidding?) then do what you must to make your winter knitting carry you through the coldest of days. Come spring and you're busy with lilacs and forsythia, clipping limbs, filling vases, transplanting; outlining the rude edge of the driveway's tar with a chaos that's worth its weight in gold.

And at your beck and call at last is summer's sun, not wasting a minute in apology for having stayed away so long. Here under this glorious blister you steal whatever hours you can to simmer and sear in only the juices most essential to you and your children, while out of your long legs, your slim arms, your nearly flat stomach, the horizon of your breasts, your face, your heart, the ache, if only temporarily, burns off and evaporates like a sauce in reduction. Basted in orange gel on your chaise in the sand at the beach by the shore, baby, you're the top; re-born invincible and immortal, nothing but blue sky and golden light, and you will feel this way forever, so help me God. If only for this moment, the atom splits for no one but you. You are radiant and clean electric. As guilty a pleasure as a spotless X ray.

But then home you go and the sun is just another planet. There's the push mower abandoned by the front path, and the noise that should have been the whir of blades is instead blunt snorts of snores coming from the screened doors and open windows. You find him in the playroom asleep sitting up, his glasses half on, half off, leaving dents in his fleshy cheeks, sweat slicking what's now more scalp than hair, and grease stains dripped in a path down his T-shirt to where the cotton has given up and his stomach has taken over. It was the last of the pickled herring you realize; the empty container leaving its own smear trail on your new coffee table.

"Dan. Dan, wake up," you say in that voice even you hate hearing, like someone took sandpaper to your vocal chords, but he doesn't hear you, so you figure what the hell, let him sleep for all you care. In between his snorts you catch assorted bits from the backyard; the squeak of the swing set's chains, Charlie's "quit it," Heidi fighting English and melody: "goink to de CHIPPLE und veer GOINK to git ma-a-a-RID." The rough lines that sunburned around your bathing-suit straps pinch as you reach for the tub on the table, and all you want to do is wash off the rest of the Ban de Soleil and slip into some Noxema, but there's the fork still in his fist with a piece of herring on it, "Daaan." And those thick, thick thighs squeezing out of those good madras shorts you got him at Paul Stuart, and his calves, and ankles, too, they look so swollen, how can they be so big? And those sores; all those sores. I can't look at them.

"Dan."

He snores.

His shoulder cap is twice what it was when you first leaned against it. You slap your palm on it like killing a bug.

"Wake up. Dan."

He snorts. His head tips south and snaps to. His eyes try to say hello.

"Are you awake?"

"Hmmm?" The hand with the fork lifts like a heavy crane to his face. "What?" He pushes his glasses into place with the back of it. "Awake?" There's a smudge of grease on the lens where he touched it. He's finally looking at you, but you have to turn away. You don't want him seeing these tears.

"I'm awake." He tries to clear his throat, but leaves something for next time.

Out back, Adam scoops Josh into the air at the base of the slide.

"OK. Huh? Yes."

SIX

Where we've been going to.

WE LIVE IN THE PAST, OR WE LIVE IN THE FUTURE, and in between we drive and drive. The old car is gone, scrap bound for the heap, and with it, little pieces of our lives, the good and the bad, left in the chasm between seat and backrest and now too late to retrieve, a knitting needle, two jacks and a buffalo nickel, Aggie's old leash, an onyx cufflink, a pop gun, a dozen more memories we don't even remember we remember and some we wish we could forget and can't.

The new car is white, bright white. White so bright for such a cloudy day like today, so new, so tomorrow, it's hard to imagine we spent five years in that red-on-black two-tone, half police cruiser, half fire engine, so new when it was new and so old when it wasn't. All that driving, to and from the station, all those weekends of groceries and hardware and piano lessons and Little League and the kosher butcher and the beach and the orchard and the skating pond and the nursery. All those dirt roads winding to all those summer cabins, and the same tires skidding in the winter up the drive. The horn the boys broke that day at the lawyer's when we left them in the car and should have known their patience wouldn't last the time it took to draw up our wills. The backseat three different litters of puppies treated like a chew toy, and, once or twice, like a fire hydrant. The axle that snapped going uphill in reverse at that antique store where we bought the Spanish chest, the hand-painted one, the one that wouldn't fit in the back, the one that was strapped to the roof in the rain, uncovered. The front right fender and headlight that broke hitting the guardrail that time on the curve up Eastly Road. That's all in the past now, growing as small and smaller in the rearview mirror as the auto dealership. Small and smaller and fainter and gone, and here we are now, a family united in a flash of white as new white as an Atlas Rocket.

We don't get to spend all that much time with the boys, and when we do, it seems we're always in the car.

Always on our way to . . . or coming back from . . . Everything always what was or what will be, both in the car and out of it, too.

We live in the past, or we live in the future, and seldom if ever do we stop and savor what's now, what's here in front of us, this minute, this second, this new car, this fried clam, this kiss, not next summer, not last winter, but right here, right now. Myrmy fills the boys' heads with "wouldn't it be wonderful if . . ." and "oh, wasn't it wonderful when . . ." confusing their moments with fragments overlapping like runny foods on a plate, everything jumbled together and no taste unique in itself.

Waiting in line for the World of Tomorrow's exhibit at the World's Fair last year, she yelled at Charlie for dripping ice cream on his shirt (the shirt he wanted to look nice in, didn't he, when we'd be visiting Nana the following weekend, remember?). Scolded him all puffy-eyed and hiccupy just as his face was next to broadcast over the picture-telephone demonstration. Or at the Model T Races at Chalk Flats last month when she reminded Josh how we used to wheel him around in a stroller not so long ago, and how nice it was that his little legs didn't have to get all tired out like they were getting now, wasn't it?

She says these things and I feel it coming up in my throat like hot soup, "shut up already, shut up with the wouldn't its and wasn't its, Goddamnit, Myrmy, shut up." But then I think I'll be the one spoiling the moment, whatever moment it is that I want her paying attention to, that I want the boys paying attention to and enjoying as it's happening, a moment that's about to become one of those nostalgic wasn't its, so I say nothing and the moment flashes by. And yet, somehow, by some divine perversion in her brain chemistry, those moments I'm convinced Myrmy's missing, Myrmy is indeed memorizing, filing them away as future wasn't its as sure as can be. And as sure as can be, the admonishments are as much a part of, and are as fondly recalled as, the not-missed-after-all moments themselves. It's quite a spin on a hairpin curve; you've got to hand it to her.

Me? I want to hold onto right now. Hold its hand tight, palm to palm so tight I can feel the blood flow between us, palm on the wheel so tight I can feel the new battery hum. Hold onto the moment as it's happening, to the experience in itself. Hold it, see it, breathe it in for what it is, and is alone. No looking forward to it becoming a memory. No thinking back to when it was only a dream on the horizon. I want now to be now, new car fresh and nothing but. And I want Adam and Charlie and Josh to know what now feels like, now for itself, pure and uninfected by contaminated clocks and calendars. Anything else, anything more ladled into any given moment is too much to swallow and only causes gagging. So the slimy pumice of a puppy's tongue on their faces, or the smell of this new station wagon, or the *hee-hee Pooh's head's in a honey pot oh bother,* there's a lifetime in such moments and they deserve to go un-interrupted for the seconds they take. There's plenty of time later for now to be then. And in case they forget, I've got most of it on Super 8.

We live in the past, or we live in the future, and in between the things that drive us are sometimes the very things we've lost along the way. Some of these we re-member we've lost, remember when we lost them even, and, oddly, where, and some we don't, and some we wish we could forget and never will.

And then there are those things that weren't even ours to lose whose loss lives on in our lives. The babies, of course, the ones Myrmy and I lost, the ones we've never spoken of to the boys, the ones only Adam would know about from memory, if he even remembers at that. Their losses are as much a part of Adam's nows, and

Charlie's, and Josh's, as if they were captured on Super 8 and looped day after day after year after year, looped on the screens in their mother's eyes and mine. Memories like these don't fall behind car seats like house keys and loose change, they don't end up as part of the whole in a scrap heap flattened like spatulas or compacted into cubes and forgotten so-what. They leap out just before impact, or trade in, and they steal their own vehicles, and they race across those screens too fast for cops to catch, screeching tires and leaving tread marks on the lam to who knows where, over and over and over again.

Every time Myrmy mummifies Charlie's neck with an extra scarf before he goes out sledding ("I don't care if it's melting, it's still cold out"), binding his neck as stiff as the saucer; every time Josh churns at the beach like an animal trapped in an invisible cage waiting to go back in the water after lunch ("a full hour, I said, and just wade where I can see you, no, closer"); every time Adam doesn't go bicycling with his friends because ("they're too wild") and ("don't you have homework?") and ("you can't play the piano with a broken wrist, you could break it, and then what would you do?"); every time she overprotects and underallows, and every time I step aside and let her, it's the loss of those babies screeching across both our screens as loud as ghostly possible. The dead fortune-telling for the living and we're the mediums.

We live in the past, or we live in the future, and who am I to tell my wife that her heartbreak is leaking, that the cranberry relish is into the gravy is into the buttered beans and the boys are getting fat on it.

She thinks I don't notice. She says that I'm the one doing the damage here, not her. Says it anywhere it pleases her, too. Lets it erupt out of her like pus.

"You're like those troops Johnson's sending over. Every day, every year that you don't go to the doctor, it's building up. And then what? God knows what, that's what."

"Bullshit."

"Yeah, that's right, bullshit. You keep saying it, Dan. Bull-shit."

"They're gonna hear you. They're just outside the office."

"I don't care if they hear me. Someone has to hear me, because clearly you don't. You can't even look at me when I'm talking to you."

"Buy another dress, Myrmy. Buy another hat. Get the UPS driver to listen to you."

"Should I buy another house, too, and another car? Oh that's right, I'm already buying this one."

"Go to hell."

"No. Here, take the keys. You drive."

———

What good does it do to dwell on the past or guess at the future if it numbs the taste buds to the moment at hand? Will Adam remember the sweet tart cool of a lemon ice mixing with the cool plastic fresh of the new car? Or only that the yellow is dribbling on the aqua Naugahyde and probably leaving a sticky spot on the brand-new imitation caning, and the trouble he'll be in because of it? Better, though, that he should remember a moment like this, a memory he alone is making, than carry with him all his life someone else's accident, reckless moments like the one in the salesman's office, what we said and the words we used. Even with the man out of the room, and the door closed, the three of them crowded all antagonistic knees and elbows into that bucket-seat chair just outside in the showroom, they had to have heard us. I kept watching Adam's head to see if he was cocking it to hear. Has he learned how to listen without looking? Has Josh?

So much of the past is so much of the future, all cause and effect, all warmed-up leftovers, all one long road like Southeast Asia, the sons fighting then fathering the sons fighting now, the nickels lost behind all those seats paying for all those new dog tags. Substitute the fathers then for their sons now, point to a Bell helicopter instead of a B-52, replace Murrow with Huntley and Brinkley and a bomb of any size still burns, and scars, and kills, and leaves wounds everlasting.

So much of my past is so much of their future, my sons, my little boys, my Adam and Charlie and Josh, my dead and buried. It's in the very skin on my neck they've learned to knead while I'm driving. To keep me awake. To keep the road ahead, ahead.

I hate that my past is so much of their now and who knows of their future. That their hands are asked to ache against their wills for wounds they had no part in. Those soft mad bones all thumbs and knuckles, sticky from Italian ices and impatient to pass the buck. It's Adam's turn. Make Josh do it. Charlie. It spoils a trip like this: the first ride in a new car. Spoils it, as much as a door ding in new chrome that they have to carry over their backseat obligation. That it's not headed for the junkyard with the rest of the left-behinds in the old car. That it's as much a part of now as then and feels like it always will be.

Oh, that I could wipe it away like the rain on the windshield, wipe it away, wipe it away. Focus on their fingertips and the histories in their touch, loop the Super 8's and live their nows as mine.

Charlie: how he swells all calcium and adrenaline with the weight of a baseball in his hand. Stitching and smooth leather exciting as a found penny to his thumb's caress. The world that ball is, perched like a diamond in a five-point setting. The world, and all its power in peaceful balance. I taught him to throw, but it's his own natural instincts that coil him into a perfect watch spring. How many little batters have wet their pants as his pitches whizzed strikes.

Adam: my Albert Einstein. He has no more affinity for a ninth-inning stretch than I have for an Oscar Peterson riff. But man, at a piano, those hands are Sandy Koufax, boy; sturdy and leaping and sliding chords-long into a B-flat on a perfect steal. Adam's veins bicker under his skin like lines of type under vellum. But soothe his head and nervous system with the balm of jazz records and encyclopedias, and his whole body flips into the "on" position.

Josh: who he is is who I am to him. A craggy hilltop, or so it feels. A solo climb without the ropes his mother throws him. I'm there. I'm looming. He'll scale me jut by jut, tentative hand by uncertain foot. Plop his behind in my lap. (He hardly fills half a thigh.) He'll cup his torso like an inchworm against my overfed stomach and rest his head on the thick mound of my chest. With his little fingers, he'll thread a cat's cradle out of my fatter ones; and he'll breathe out little puffs on my gray chest hairs like they're dense dandelion balls. Does he feel my heart jump under that little cheek? Does he know that as I snatch for air I smell him all tapioca? Only when Sunday tears have glistened for no good reason, or weeknight tantrums filled that little mouth with words too big for its own good, words he hasn't heard from me, does he have reason to skulk about me like a cat, and stay off my summit. One day, he'll plant his flag on me. Take those little fingers that poke at my neck and wrap them around the pole and plant it. Claim me for his very own. One day.

"Dan, watch the road—it's slick."

"I'm watching, I'm watching."

"Shvelbeles, you love the car? Won't it be nice when we go to the Cape? Hmmm? Adam? What's that on the seat?"

We live in the past, and the past is the future, and whether we shift into drive or go in reverse or throw it in park now to stop at Carroll's for hamburgers, every moment that ever was is right here with us, along for the ride, where it's been and where it's headed all slopped together one long loop in Super 8. The good and the bad, left in the chasm between seat and backrest and now too late to retrieve, a knitting needle, two jacks and a buffalo nickel, Aggie's old leash, an onyx cufflink, a pop gun, a dozen more memories we don't even remember we remember and some we wish we could forget and can't. What good would going to a doctor now do? It's all there with us all the time all new-car fresh, so new when it's new, and as new when it's not.

SEVEN

Something in the air.

---

cMARY FENCE HOSTESSED A LUNCHEON.

Not on a Saturday, when Dan could have easily, easily taken charge of the errands and the boys (taken the boys with him to the Food Fair and Barker's and Caldor's and the Factory Store); nor on a Sunday, when, again, Dan could have equally easily, easily seen to it that Sheila made her train into the city for her day off (where she gets to speak her Spanish to people who can say more back to her than "is breakfast ready?"), and seen to it that the boys got to and from Sunday school, and Adam and Josh to and from their piano lessons after and Charlie to his guitar lesson (assuming that his teacher regained consciousness from his night before). No, Mary hostessed a luncheon not over the weekend, not on a Saturday nor on a Sunday but on a Friday, wouldn't you know, a work-day for those of us who work.

It was a luncheon for "the girls": me, Mary of course, Pauline Drucker, Mae Swoon, Dorothy Waxler, and Evelyn Lenz. Five Jews and Mary (who's so Catholic at times it hurts). A Friday luncheon for "the girls." She's been calling us that ever since we all became friends, of sorts, after I first met their husbands on the train and later when our children were all in nursery school together, more or less at the same time, and we were all on baking committees and chaperoning adventures to Nyala Farms, also on days when those of us who work had to save face by not doing so, so the children could learn where the milk they spill comes from. We've all stayed friends, if you want to call it that, some of us closer than others, but none of us straying too far from the pack lest our reputations suffer the consequences.

We all attend the same cocktail parties and we're more or less a group, not entirely Mary McCarthy–like, much to Mary's disappointment. Though, press her on the mat-ter and she'd be the first to confess relief that there's not a lesbian in the bunch (that we know of), and definitely not Clare Booth Luce–like, this is the woods after all and not Park Avenue, and, besides, we all have the same husbands we started with (if you don't count Pauline's little-talked-about *gaffe d'amour*, as Dorothy refers to it like clockwork midway into her second vodka Collins), but a group we are, I guess you could say, yes, we are, we're a group.

We've watched each other's children fall off jungle gyms and we've referred one another to nondenominational summer camps where for four weeks the children can pretend they're indians and make ashtrays, and we've howled about run-ins with Dr. Sneer, the pediatrician (suggestive nomenclature not lost on that one). We bump carts now and then at the 5 & 10, and, once in a great while, I see them at the far end of the train station when they make rare appearances on the platform, wobbling onto it in their dress-up heels as cautiously as cats who know they shouldn't be on the kitchen counter, on their ways to cultural outings in the city (although why anyone would want to shimmy into a girdle and schlep into the city when they didn't have to . . .)

We're a group, and Mary was hostessing a luncheon just for us. On a Friday. So, no fool I, I took the day (what choice did I have?) off (with pay) because there would be no way in the universe that I would be the absentee guest they all talked about (and I know they talk about me plenty because I talk about them. At work.).

As it turned out, however, my fears were for naught.

"Evelyn rsvp-ed she'd be here," Mary said, confirmed

"in a very strange voice," Mary added, "very late, I might add, on Tuesday night," Mary said additionally (in a voice that was one foot shy of being inside a confessional). Yet for the duration of the luncheon, Evelyn's blonde, Scandinavian dining chair went empty, and her serving of lox-and-tuna-melt supreme with a cole slaw side wound up congealed in the dog's dish, and her phone remained busy the entire afternoon, every time Mary tried the number. So naturally, with Evelyn God-knows-where, we talked about her.

Her, and the item in the paper.

Not the sort you'd want your friends reading as they scooped their husbands' morning grapefruit, but . . .

Suffice it to say, as far as the article Mae couldn't wait to brandish and read to us, it read:

"'Arthur Samuel Lenz, Regional Manager at International Bottle . . .'"

"He's a Manager? Walter's been there longer . . ."

"'. . . has removed himself . . .'"

"(removed himself . . . ?)"

"'. . . from his home at 28 Wagonberry Lane . . .'"

"(Or been removed . . . ?)"

"Dorothy, will you let me read? '. . . due to a domestic matter dubbed "alienation of affections . . ."'"

"Been removed."

Big inhale from Mary.

"'. . . a charge brought upon him by Evelyn Finkleburg Lenz . . .'"

"Oy, Mary, Mother of Christ . . ."

"'. . . his wife of seventeen years . . .'"

"Seventeen? What was she, twelve, when they got married?"

"'. . . in her petition for divorce . . .'"

"Divorce!"

Frantic sign of the Cross (practically a flagellation), from Mary.

"'. . . Named as corespondent is . . .' (oh, you're not going to believe this) '. . . is a . . .'"

"Who?"

"Who?"

"Whom?"

"May I finish, please? '. . . a Miss Sukie Jones . . .'"

"Who?"

"I'm getting to that. '. . . a Miss Sukie Jones of 12 Puffin Street, Eastport . . .'

"Puffin Street? Oh, Puffin Street. Eastport. Near the station . . ."

"Pau . . . '. . . the Lenz' now-former babysitter . . .'"

"Aah!"

"How do you like that? And she told me she didn't have a regular babysitter she could recommend."

"'. . . and a recent graduate of Button Gwynneth High School, Eastport . . .'"

"I knew it. Myrmy, didn't I tell you something was fishy?"

"'. . . As of Wednesday morning last . . .'"

"You did? Where was I?"

"Mary, do you ever turn the heat on in here?"

"Oh, I know, but Ed likes the chill. Makes him cough less, he says."

"'. . . As of Wednesday morning last,' Pauline . . . '. . . As of Wednesday morning last, Mr. Lenz has been residing at the Yankee Doodler Motel on Route 3 in Eastport . . .'"

"A hop, skip, and a jump rope away from that flower child, no doubt."

"Puffin Street? Where near the station is that?"

"Oh, you know, it's near . . . it's near . . . Dorothy, what's the name of that knitting store . . . ?"

"The Darn Yarn Barn?"

"Right. It's . . . it's near there."

"Pauline, since when do you knit?"

"I knit, Mae, OK? Phil travels."

"Evelyn. Hmmm. (I wonder if she'll keep the house.)"

"Didn't she just redecorate? In greens?"

"If she did, maybe you should cancel your new drapes, Mae. Could be a bad omen."

"Girls, pumpkin éclairs?"

———

The boys still ask after Nettie. Have I heard from her? Does she think about them? Will she ever come back? Three years ago, fifty-eight years of laundry and dishes and rag mops and silver polish and other women's households finally caught up with her thick knees and coatrack shoulders, and love the boys though she did, her body just couldn't keep pace with her heart. How they cried themselves to sleep the night before she left (Josh, the most, Charlie, less so, Adam, least, from fighting it), those carbonated sobs ("Don't go! Don't go!") dampening pillowcases a new housekeeper would be washing. (And the ones after those by the ones after her.) And Nettie's tears, too. A mother's tears for the children she loved as well as her own and maybe better. Thick tears in rivulets backing up like a plugged drain on her glasses' lower rims as she packed her few day-off dresses (those faded florals so like my own mother's), and packed last the suite of white lace curtains I gave her as a going-away gift ("Oh, Mizzuz, oh my . . .") for the house she built, yet only her husband had lived in, while she spent her years in white starched uniforms north of the Mason-Dixon line.

It was better for the children, so much better that she should leave on an early train on a Saturday morning before they woke up, better that she should already be on her way south when they sat down to breakfast, eggs and bacon and pancakes instead of the grits she liked to make for them, Dan serving up enough food to distract them as I drove home from seeing her off on the platform and crying our good-byes, the only two women there so early (me in my latest new coat and she in my latest old), wet cheeks suctioned together and hugging so tight I felt our colors blend like cream into coffee.

Better, too, that too much time shouldn't pass between Nettie's going and the next one's coming. (Frances, was it? Or Ula? Serrita? Who came before Heidi?) Whoever it was, she arrived the next day on the afternoon express, giving me just enough time before doing my nails and laying out my clothes for the morning (and the boys'), to show her where the washer was, and the broom and the mop, and which meats were labeled what in the freezer down in the garage, and how to polish the brass faucets in my bathroom, and as I watched three sets of owl eyes watch her watch me I pointed out the numbers listed by the kitchen phone for my office and Dan's and the pediatrician and the school and the fire department, and told her what day the milk came, and what day the garbage went, and what to do when UPS was picking up or dropping off, and does she know how to use a rectal thermometer and be careful here at the stove that you don't leave a burner on with the paper towels hanging right there and that's pot roast for tonight (Dan, are you watching this?) and the agency told you it's Thursdays and every other Sunday off, (right?) and I can't think of anything else now the dogs get half a can each mixed with kibble twice a day and the cats get fed outside there's canned milk in the cabinet to the left and Friskies under the sink the boys'll show you we're up very early and there's chicken for tomorrow night make sure you take it out first thing so it thaws the boys can have cereal for breakfast do you have any questions?

———•———

"I wonder how Evelyn will cope."

"Rattling around in that big house."

"Assuming she gets to keep it."

"I sincerely doubt she will."

"She won't. With a second Mrs. Lenz queuing up, Arthur's sure to insist they sell."

"He's a foxy one, you know."

"Apparently, foxier than we knew."

"Foxier *and* friskier."

"'The quick brown fox'... how does that go?"

"Oh right, from typing class."

"I took stenography, you know."

"Good thing Gene rescued you from the shallow end of the steno pool."

"I was good!"

"Are you still?"

"What is Evelyn going to do? Get a job?"

"It's not the end of the world. Some of us do it."

"Maybe *you*. But what normal person would want to get into a girdle at 5:30 every morning?"

"We can't all spend our lives sitting around in Bermuda shorts bloating on stingers, now can we?"

"Can't you see her in an interview? 'I went to Vassar. I majored in van Gogh. I can make vichyssoise.' She's doomed!"

"Don't forget, she has Kevin and Rhonda to think about."

"Kevin'll wind up in juvenile hall, you just wait."

"He did not burn your barn down, Mae, it was lightning."

"It was Kevin."

"She'll get plenty of alimony, you'll see."

"Even Arthur thinks he did it."

"All right, all right . . ."

"And Evelyn isn't exactly the most attentive mother now, what's this going to do?"

"Should I try to call her again? Tell her we're here for her?"

———•———

What a difference a pronoun makes. From "ours" to "mine," from "we" to "I," from "us" to "me." On a Wednesday morning Evelyn went from seventeen years of thinking of herself in the plural (and I don't mean in the royal sense), to smashing head-on into I-me-my without a seat belt. And Arthur, Arthur got to leave the scene of the accident scratch-free and we-us in tact, in fact absconded with Evelyn's we-us as brazenly as if he were a mugger stealing her diamond ring, snatched that we-us out from under her while she wasn't even looking and delivered it on a silver-plated platter to little miss Sukie soon-to-be Mr.'s new Mrs. us-we Lenz.

In the confusion, fresh as it is, I'm sure Evelyn is trip-
ping over "I" and "us" as if they were sleeping cats in a
darkened hallway, only it's her lungs tearing the air upon
each misfooting. What half of a whole (the half being left,
that is, not the half doing the leaving) can be expected to
instantly modify her vocabulary when she first has to get
over the shock of watching her favorite words elope to
the next town and move into another woman's mouth
without any say in the matter? And, for that matter, little
miss babysitter is in for a rude shock if she thinks tran-
sitioning from I-me-my to us-we-Mrs. will be no more
complicated than throwing on a strand of love beads and
saying "groovy." At her young age, at any age really, I doubt
she's any more prepared to soon take on a pronoun than
Evelyn is now to divorce one, or Mrs. King was to have
just buried one. I-me-my-mine-we-us-ours, they seem
such little words, but how enormous the difference.

And how enormous the difference in the sequence
of them. From single girl to suddenly "us," an overnight "we" plumping "our" cushions, does little miss
home wrecker reckon it's all going to be tenderness
and redeemable green stamps? Does she fully grasp the
concept of "for better or for worse?" Is she capable of
understanding that "worse" sometimes comes dressed as

"better?" When her hankering for an electric can opener (just because), (just for instance) gets shelved in favor of the ten-cup chrome-plated percolator Arthur likes the sound of better, and assures her she'll be happier with (even though it's no skin off his index finger with each crank on the cans of canned peas) she'll want to throw those plump pillows flat, burst their seams, and free the "me" of each trapped feather. And while those are "their" cushions, "he" bought them, and it will have been "his" money, too, that paid for those groceries the sheet of stamps came with. And although "she" will have licked them, it's "he" who holds the book of them.

Flip the page, and seventeen years of collective identity, good or bad, and only Evelyn can say which it was (although, knowing Arthur and the vulgar way he advertises himself in too tight tennis whites I'd say more of the latter), seventeen years of it suddenly lobbed over the net at her in a wad of legal papers may be the ruder order of things. Drop the "s" from the "us" and all you're left with is little old lonely "u."

———·———

If Dan and I were to divorce (and don't think I haven't thought of it), he'd be the one with the bigger language problem. Tumbling from "we" to "me" for him, I think, would be leaving the service all over again, a Company C man out of his tailored uniforms and into civvies, civvies that went out of fashion and no longer fit. It can't be easy for him, I realize that, as part of my "we." He started out such a capital "I" and he's become so lowercase. Or did I only imagine him in the upper? Hope he was the upper? Tell myself he was the upper that could stand tall against my own ascending capitalization? We're so much a "we" on my doing, year after year more and more the slower he goes. And if he went? I'd still be "I," the "I" that is "us," the "I" that has had no choice but to be "us" for the boys' sakes and for my own (and say it out loud I haven't the heart), for his more than anyone's.

Being the one who leaves is the one to be. The adulterer off for greener pastures. The steno pool-er who washes her hands of the take-a-memo-life and dries them on new his-and-hers towels. The retiree. The dead.

Lose the claim check on purpose and let the dry cleaning yellow on the shop's carousel, a voice from within calls out to them. There's a new and improved way out of Sanforized lives and Hollanderized loves and the brave aren't afraid to breathe in its fumes.

Dan did it, once. Marched away from a wife he no

longer loved, or who no longer loved him, or both, or neither cared which; a wife who was content with her fancy hats and her hup-to husband and wanted no children to come between either. So he packed his foot lockers and his duffels and his dobb kit and his gun, and he was done with her; shave and a haircut and he was out the door, because he was still young and robust and there was more to have and he'd find her. Arthur's found her (in pigtails, under Evelyn's nose), Phil Drucker found her (as much of a find as one might call Pauline, who claims she's blonde because she's Norwegian. Norwegian Jews? I'm sorry . . .). Countless men on the train find her every day, outside their offices, their buildings, their lives. Out with the old and in with the new and improved, they cry. Better than a laundered shirt, a new one, they sing. No cuffs fraying, or buttons loose, or telltale signs of too little antiperspirant too late where the armpits are permanently hued amber. Unpin the neck, snake out the collar's cardboard yoke, shake out the new broadcloth with a snap and run a cool iron over the creases as needed, and hello morning. Hang your conscience on the carousel and let the claim checks fall where they may.

At least Dan had the good grace not to find her before he closed that door. At least he bulled his way down the stoop with a new we-us just an idea keeping his hopeful head high, an idea that had no children going wanting for his lips on their bedtime brows.

Not like Arthur, leaving Evelyn to cope with a hooligan and a disappearing daughter, the more she eats the less she weighs (whoever heard of that?).

And not like my father, who went off to his pharmacy one day and didn't come home, no "I'll be late," no "don't wait up," no "kiss baby Muriel good night for me."

"Hissed his usual good-for-nothing something to mother," my grandmother would hiss.

"Punched his arms into his overcoat and tore a sleeve's lining, ripped it clean out," my uncles would report.

"Left without his lunch tin, that was a surprise," my aunts would add.

"I came up to see what's what and there were his pickled eggs and your mother said eat and I said his eggs and she yeah and I said *nu*," the downstairs widow would cluck, tucking tissues under her brassiere each time.

"Let her cry," my mother said she said for nights on end. "She thinks he's coming home. He's not. She'll cry. She'll stop."

"Said she said it for nights on end for months on end," I laughed to psychiatrist diploma after psychiatrist diploma.

"Said she wouldn't even come in to soothe me in my crib," I raged to ceiling tile after ceiling tile.

"Said she thought it was better this way," I cried into cold leather couch after cold leather couch.

"Is that why I never loved him" I whispered to wet handkerchief after wet handkerchief.

"Is that why I didn't cry when he died" I asked compact mirror after compact mirror.

"Is that why I could kill them all for what they did," I still say, straightening stocking seam after stocking seam.

"Scribble scribble scratch period," I hear pen-and-pad after pen-and-pad reply.

———

Retell the bits and pieces of life enough times and they all reduce down to their own special shorthand, becoming the briefest of parenthetical asides. (My first wife), (the old car), (my father), (the babies), (Nettie). Each its own steno flick on a ruled page, each its own snarked mark standing in for more words than you can bear to repeat. But repeat them we do. In our heads, in our hearts, in our dreams the full text of them blossom like pollen to an asthmatic, the saddest anecdotes the hardiest, crowding out the soft touch, the day pretty, gilding the edges of even the happiest recall in nicotine yellow. Till the day she's buried (my ex-husband), will be the aside Evelyn's memory gossips about with the most glee, turns right to that page and reads right back to her, through teeth with food in them.

Let it go, people say.

Enough already, Dan says.

Quit it, the boys say.

"Myrmy," Dorothy says, eyes as low as her drink.

"You're being awfully quiet," Mae says, her small chin hiding behind the words.

"For a change," Pauline says, her Norwegian pageboy (and its Sheep's Head Bay roots) stiff as a fjord.

"I feel terrible for Evelyn, too," Mary leans in to say to me softly. Her fingernails are short and unpolished, unashamed of mothering. On my hand her hand is Pop-n-Fresh warm. I let it linger long enough not to offend, then slip mine out for a Salem.

"If he doesn't want to be there, he doesn't want to be there. What would you have her do," I say, "tell him not to go? Beg him to love her again? Like an old hobby?"

"She shouldn't just let him go like that," Dorothy says to Pauline's concurring nods. "She should make it difficult."

She should make it difficult.

Like my mother made it difficult.

She didn't want her man, or any man, and he didn't want her, but she didn't want him free to want someone else.

"She should give him his *get* and get it over with," I say, as surely no one in my mother's circle said to her. Mary blindly gropes to comprehend me, all quizzical mouth and no eyes, like a new kitten searching for a nipple, so I tutor: "It's a Jewish divorce. Think Vatican annulment, but you don't have to pay for it. Up front." She nods, she shakes her head, it'll come off one of these days, and I can tell that were the five us beads on a chain, she'd be 'Our Father-ing' us with trembling fingers, devout fingers, mumbling love.

———

"You all are in my prayers," Nettie said there on the platform. "Every night, before I close my eyes, I ask Him to bless you, every one."

I wanted to give her my mink stole, and the big pearl ring, and cast her in gold for a charm on my bracelet, keep the sound of her with me, with the children.

"How we'll miss you. You don't know how we'll miss

you," I said there, just the two of us, the catch in my throat hanging like wash on the line. How much I missed her already.

"I know, Mizzuz. I know."

"I know you know." And I knew she knew.

And I know she knew how how much I missed her already was wrapped up in how much I'd missed. How saying good-bye to her was saying good-bye to times with the children that only she knew, and that I know about only anecdotally from what she told me evening after evening, workday after workday. Tears that I never dried, gasps of new discovery—a frog! an arrowhead!— random afternoon memories of them that I don't have and she'll have always.

My career is words and she can't read, and her career is my children and she's taking the notes with her. And it's all there all around us on the platform, down the tracks, in the air like the forecast of snow.

I want to thank her for living my life for me, for loving my children, but instead of the words, instead of the words, we embrace. And it's my idea first.

"Take care of them little ones for me," she said then, she says now, I'll always hear her saying. "And you take care of your*self*."

In my chest, in my throat, in the back of my closet, behind my wedding album and under the pillows of my crib there are words stillborn: *Don't go. Don't go.*

———

And there's Evelyn's empty blonde, Scandinavian dining chair sitting among us saying nothing, saying everything, as we all scratch Mary's floor pushing our own chairs away from the table, crumbs tumbling, napkins witness-marked with lipsticks, like Nettie's cheek with mine.

Thank yous at the door.

A chorus of "I'll call yous" and a lone, "I still say it was Kevin," from Mae.

It's late, and Mary has dishes to do before her girls come home from school.

EIGHT

On the surface of things.

$\mathcal{S}$EPT. 24, 1968

2:15 a.m.

Patient admitted to ER, complaining of severe back and chest distress, obstructed breathing, accelerated heartbeat, high fever, chills, paroxysmal cough with minor incidence of blood-colored expectoration, head and general body aches, sore throat, extreme fatigue.

2:26 a.m.

Patient requests wheelchair during in-take, informed of unavailability at this time.

Patient requests Spouse locate wheelchair. Spouse detained.

2:27 a.m.
Patient faints.

2:29 a.m.

Patient revived without medical assist.

Wheelchair delivered.

2:33 a.m.

Patient delivered in wheelchair to examining bay F by Orderly.

2:42 a.m.

Patient examined by Nurse.

Temperature 103°

Blood pressure 130/80

Pulse 56, arrhythmia noted.

Arrhythmia congenital, Patient informs.

Blood panel 8cc draw.

Vials dropped by Nurse.

Complaint lodged.

Blood panel 8cc re-draw. Patient belligerent.

3:08 a.m.

Patient examined by Attending and Resident. Labored breathing observed. Also, deep chest cough with traces of rusty sputum. Presence of fluid in both lungs detectable under stethoscopic exam. Lips cracked and sere, indicating dehydration. Back pain determined consistent with lower lung inflammation. Pupils dilated. Throat red, ulcerations noted.

Chest X rays ordered.

Patient exhibits signs of anxiety: excess perspiration, breathing shallow and accelerated.

3:28 a.m.

Patient transported to Radiology.

Complaint of "recklessness" on part of Orderly under investigation.

3:57 a.m.

Chest and back X rays photographed.

Patient lachrymose.

4:12 a.m.

Patient returned to examining bay F.

Patient agitated.

10cc Phenobarbital ordered by Attending and prepped.

Patient's breathing extremely labored.

2 litres O_2 administered. Double intubation.

4:20 a.m.

Patient's breathing unchanged.

O_2 increased to +4 litres

4:29 a.m.

Call placed to Radiology requesting Patient's X rays per Patient's request.

4:37 a.m.

Patient loses consciousness.

Blood pressure 120/90

Pulse 54

Temperature 104.2°

4:41 a.m.

Patient regains consciousness.

Speech incoherent. Requests that Spouse "call home and wake the children to see if they are asleep."

5:06 a.m.

Call placed to Radiology requesting Patient's X rays per Attending's request.

5:29 a.m.

X rays delivered to Attending and Resident. Reviewed by same.

Per review, Patient's condition classified:

Acute Double Pneumonia.

5:41 a.m.

Patient transferred to ICU.

5:46 a.m.

Patient's Spouse located in waiting room, awakened and advised of Patient's condition.

5:48 a.m.

Patient delivered to ICU, isolation bed 4.

Patient tented.

O_2 +8 litres.

Saline IV 1000cc

Temperature 104.2°

Patient's cough paroxysmal, semi-productive with rusty sputum. Breathing extremely constricted.

6:06 a.m.

Patient loses consciousness.

Blood pressure 120/70

Pulse 57

6:07 a.m.

Crash cart ordered on stand-by.

6:09 a.m.

Patient's Spouse gowned and admitted to ICU.

Patient's Spouse informed by Attending of Patient's unstable condition. Alerted to strong possibility of further conditional degeneration, as current status indicates.

Patient's Spouse advised by Attending to contact Clergy of choice, if so desired.

You want to love someone.

It's in you like blood and bone, the desire. Circulating as sure as blood, and as solid a weight as bone it's heavy in you, and permanent. You don't have to do much to give life to the want. Breathe and you feel its suck from time before time, long before amoeba, and maybe, matter before it. With no human effort it begins coagulating about you before you're you, coating every particle of every helix that God's decided you'll be.

Long before you're you, and alive, and alone, you know you don't want to be alone. The atom feels it as a longing, this want, the cell as an ache. Deep in you the ache, an ache with a mission, a compass-less mission propelling you out into feelings unthinkable, space with no North Star, eyes blinkered in search of the you for me.

Movies don't steer you right. Nor books. Nor TV commercials, they're the worst at giving directions. Make me love-able so someone will love me, make me pretty/virile/steel-belted/pine-scented and I'll be the one they want is the wrong cry to sell to sleeping hearts. The balm isn't liquid on a roll-on ball, isn't cylinders under a hood, available in fine stores everywhere. Desire can't fill out a shopping list as easy as all that. The aching urge is the product itself, an invention in search of a use, and a user. Public domain it is; no patent, no copyright, but each of us feels it as if no one else could. Beating its fists and yelling till it's hoarse: I want to come out. Let me come out. I have to come out.

I want to love someone.

———

Was it only six weeks ago you looked across your coffee cup and thought you recognized someone you once knew? Behind the dust mites orbiting in the cigarette smoke as it joined the morning sun, as the sun joined the two of you at the breakfast table, caught in her eyes an out-of-the-corner-of-your-eyes flash of mutual recognition?

The boys were still at summer camp, three weeks in with one to go, and you were a couple once again, for a moment at least. She was doused in a perfume you couldn't recall, you remember it because you couldn't recall it, lemon but not, and the difference it made in her made all the difference to you. Her mouth wasn't sewn at the edges, not tight in it usual way, and the smoke she exhaled seemed silk from her lips, not dragon fire but baby breaths. She liked your new tie. ("Those colors look good on you," she said.) Your belt pinched less because she said so. She filled two cups with the instant crystals and poured the kettle into both, added the Half &

Half to yours first and stirred yours first before dipping the spoon into her own, and that sun hitting the spoon just right after she lifted it out stroked the wet stainless sterling. She knows you don't take Saccharin and, today, didn't ask, didn't ask any more than she used to not ask if you took sugar, because she learned you didn't, and she wanted you to know she remembered: you were the one who didn't take sugar in his coffee. Looked up and across the table at you with clean eyes and her mind wasn't on work, wasn't on children, wasn't a question, or an answer, you could tell. It was calm, calm as if after passion, when the heart's so full it can't eat another bite and the mind takes "no" for an answer. A calm you're not so sure she's ever again fully worn since that morning in the apartment with the sun streaming in like now, planks of it through the blinds across the bed and the two of you in it as one, across the hairs on your arm glowing them brass and bronze as they tickled her copper nipples, across the smooth of her knees and yours behind hers, stuck from the sweat. That morning when she wanted daylight to see how hungry she had been for a man like you. Roses she smelled of, roses after a heavy rain when you couldn't hold her any tighter or push into her any deeper, when you were both so full it hurt. That morning. That morning after that night she left her mother's mother's house with you, when she came home with you and said "to hell with them, I'm moving in with you," and she said, without any prompting from God, "I love you. I love you. Do you hear me? Only you." That lightness to her then that came back from who knows where, back with a zest of lemon to catch up over coffee, that lightness made the morning's humidity bearable and the day ahead brief prelude to night, and maybe . . .

Yet, here she is a blip later, hooked up, plugged in, tented, out. Your collar isn't even buttoned, but it's tight around your neck. You can't breathe any better than she can, but you can and it's killing you that you can. You have to call the house. You have to wake Ingerlil and tell her to tell the boys before they go to school that you didn't leave early for the train, didn't leave early without saying good-bye. You had to come to the hospital. You had to bring Mummy to the hospital because she's sick. Mummy's very, very sick. No, wait, don't tell them that. I'll tell them that. Goddamnit, hello, hello . . . ?

———

They say we'll land on the moon next summer. Say it as if it's as ordinary as going to the store for milk. We'll take off from Earth and course through heaven and pull up to a lunar crater, keep the engine running we won't be a minute. We can't breathe on the moon any better than the Soviets can, but we're going to be the first to not breathe in all those gaseous elements, all that star dust, we're going to be the first if it kills us.

But what would we do, oh, what-would-we-do if the Soviets beat us to it? If after all this time all these years of thinking we were going to go first, if after all this time all these years of planning for it, knowing it as if it were something one could know for sure, if after all this time and all these years the one who wasn't supposed to go went, got there first, kicked moon dirt in our faces . . . Comrades, how could you? How dare you? And, now, how-will-we-explain-this to America?

———·———

"How sick is Mummy," Adam wants to know. "Is it pneumonia? Last night she said her chest hurt when she coughed, and her back, too. That's pneumonia, isn't it?"

Ingerlil has dinner started. But the smell of it is airy, not earthen. Not done.

I tell him it is, "yes, you're right, it is," but I don't tell him more, fence off the ugly part of the truth with my jaw. He'll guess at it. I know he will. He's Adam.

"It's really bad pneumonia, isn't it," he says in a rush, too soon to be a question and too firm to be a guess.

The mail is stacked on the kitchen pass-through, the Con Ed bill on top, my name misspelled, again. Does someone there type in Danel instead of Daniel by candlelight?

Adam's eyes are lake glass, the way they get when he doesn't want the tears to break ranks. In them are Josh and Charlie, behind me on either side, motionless as planets.

The Lord & Taylor bill. The Bonwit Teller bill. The Bergdorf Goodman bill. All couples. All Myrmy's.

Indian summer is on us, but the heat from the day doesn't loiter once the sun recedes. The after-chill has come indoors, and it's chastising me for having been too lazy to put the storm windows back on. I can feel it; even with the sweat seeping under my arms, I can feel it.

"The doctors aren't sure yet," I say, rifling the mail as best one can with clammy hands, the full words full on to Adam first, the ghost of them to Josh and Charlie as I look up from the mortgage statement and turn to include the two.

"When will they know," Adam says, "are they doing tests," he says.

"Yes, Adam, yes," I tell him, "yes, tests," I say. Charlie's guitar teacher is raising his lesson fee.

To Charlie: "Did you practice today?" I turn back to Adam before Charlie's slack jaw strums an excuse.

"She's on medicine," I say.

"And oxygen," Adam says, "is she on oxygen?" His questions are cough syrup, bitter spoonfuls shoved in.

"Yes, Adam, she's on oxygen," I tell him, I finally tell him. "They're taking good care of her."

Adam knows when an answer is not an answer. His straight A's come from being prepared, from reading top to bottom, left to right, front and back, like her. Something in the way I check my watch, something in the way I remove my glasses and wipe them clean, circle after circle, his eyes following the cloth back into my pants pocket, his upper teeth tap-dancing on his protruding lowers as he studies the frames dropping into my shirt pocket and not going back on my face, something in all of it must say to him the answer isn't textbook, that look of his says so.

Charlie cuts to the chase. "Can we see her?"

"When are you going back," Adam trumps.

Charlie's question has none of Adam's tug-of-war urgency, none of its punch. If I say it, Charlie buys it; he's mine. Adam is more his mother's, much as he fights the claim on him. He wants to be mine, but me on her terms—me as her, yet me. He's old enough to see things as they are. Bless him his optimism, or is it a dare, that I could pull off that magic act.

"I'm going back as soon as we eat," I say, hoping Ingerlil has done something with the chicken that resembles food. The oven door squeaks open as if on cue. But the nutmeg and bleach odor coming from the kitchen now doesn't bode well.

"I want to go," Charlie says, rolling his spine against the edge of the door jamb like a vine tightening its grip, his eyes not so much on me as not on Adam.

"Aren't we going, too?" Adam says, looking from me to Josh and back again. Josh needs a haircut. Even with his eyes low in slices, his bangs butt them. In the chandelier's light, he looks like her.

How happy they always were when I used to return from business trips, when I still took business trips, when I still could. My overcoat wouldn't be down an arm before they'd cluster around me like stars, mommy-only days at end and daddy-gravity drawing them to my face for kisses, and to my pockets for the loot they knew I'd have, Sen-Sen and Chiclets and LifeSavers.

"Daddy," Josh says, "can't we go with you?"

In front of me, below me, my fingers and his hair

intertwine as I brush his bangs from his eyes. In front of me, below me, his face is in shadow. My body is blocking the light from the light. I'm an eclipse.

Before I can stall on my own, Ingerlil turns the dining room blonde, her fine-spun hair flyaway as she sets the table. Plates, silverware, paper towels. "Are we out of napkins," I ask her, "paper napkins?" She shrugs a hunk of blonde from her shoulder. As she does, the ribs on her blue turtleneck stretch across her breasts and thin out translucent, hinting at a pink bra.

"Yes?" she informs me.

And: "Dinner you will eat?"

Her guess is as good as mine.

"We are, aren't we," Adam says, again his eyes on Josh. This time, neither a question nor a guess, not so firm, not so sure. Not on his face. Not on Josh's.

And Ingerlil again: "I take train to city tomorrow?"

Yes or no, Daddy.

"Thursday?"

Answer it, Daddy.

"Day off?"

Are we going to see Mummy, Daddy?

"Tomorrow? No!" Josh says, eyes wide now under a returned veil of bangs. Ingerlil's mock-pout is meant to reassure, Josh's arms around her waist are meant to anchor, her hand on his shoulder is meant to comfort, but we're just a stop on the road for her, little man, so be careful how you cling.

I check my watch again, compare it to what the daisy over the kitchen sink reads. Five o'clock.

The dogs bark out back in their run, Jazzbo's ruff, Aggie's riff. One of the cats must have edged up to the fence, made their world seem off its axis.

5:01.

We'd be just now leaving our offices for the train, the two of us, coming home to the boys and the mail and the dogs.

"Sit," I say. "Let's eat. Charlie. Josh? Sit down. Sit."

"When can we see her," Charlie asks his milk.

"Soon," I tell his glass. "Soon."

I won't stay through dinner. I'll leave before they've made their food as murky as my answers, before they've forked and knifed out every last air pocket, sulked their meal unrecognizable. Who can blame them the blur of lumped rice and chicken shreds, in their great big help-ings of soon?

It's all rights and lefts on the way to Charmington Hospital. Rights down main roads and lefts down back ones, stoplights and stop signs and no outlets and yields, flashing reds and flashing yellows and deaf children playing. Back roads I've bumped down a hundred times at least since Ed Fence mapped them out over a dozen autumns ago seem alien, as if I'd only ever known them from the safe end of a telescope. Was that cottage always yellow? Has that curve always come so soon? Is this the spot Ed said to watch out for?

The main roads take new eyes, too. Queen Anne after Victorian after Greek Revival after Federal, houses so enormous in scale today but in their times so cozy, as she would say, collapsing in on themselves one after another down Gloanstowne Turnpike. On the right, we have Ionic columns buckling from dry rot under a sagging porte cochère. Notice on your left a leaded-glass transom popping panes as its sash disintegrates. And those eyebrow dormers there, no wonder they droop so close to closed. Out over jungled lawns where families once played horseshoes and croquet they now only gaze on the plywood backsides of real estate signs for commercial development. *4 Prime Acres! Desirable Location! Build to Suit!*

Have they always hidden their humiliation behind arthritic lilacs and monkey puzzles grown amok? How do you not notice what's there to be noticed: a turret, a cupola, a widow's walk?

Did anyone at any time in any of those homes ever dream that the day would come when such solid grandeur could decompose, when such elegance could be bulldozed, or does it always just hit out of the blue like an asteroid?

———

Ed Fence, dead from cancer for over a year now, didn't linger or sputter in a drawn-out good-bye. His wife told mine he woke one morning to a thicker cough than usual, lit his first cigarette of the new day and exhaled blood. Two weeks of tests later the doctors told him his skinny lungs were shot, and two weeks later still stubbed out his last smoke of the night and conked. Just like that.

Snap, you're out.

———

Snap, you're awakened, holding your wife's cold fingers in your warm ones, your arm punctured through a blank in the hospital bed's rail much as the intravenous line feeding her wrist, abrupt and necessary. She sleeps. Inside her oxygenated tent her face is moon pale, sinking into itself, mouth and jowls sliding down toward the pillow, cheeks scooped out like old ice cream, her nose a lonely bone. Around her eyes and mouth are lines that are new to you. On her brow, creases that weren't there a night ago, or you just didn't notice. Perhaps she's hidden them from you same as from the world. The lipstick, the false eyelashes, the shadow, the rouge, the pyrotechnics that you complain make you late getting to the station and finding a parking spot, you've always written them off as silly fashion, vanity, even though you like how it all looks on her. The lines, the creases, the crow's feet, she has kept them hidden from you, you see that now, and hidden from herself, yes maybe even more from herself than from you. But not out of vanity. Knowing her, not hidden from either of you out of vanity, but out of pride. She lets you know how angry she is, how frustrated, she says it with words, luxuriates in the venom she puts into those words. And she'll sigh her Atlas sigh. Slump her shoulders. Tell you of her throbbing head. But let you see the actual toll on her face? She won't give the world that satisfaction. How it must eat at her that it is eating at her—that the feelings are showing through her body, denting her from the inside out with a fist mightier than natural aging. Aging she can accept, rue it, fight it, put a new color on it, because what other choice does anyone have beyond plastic surgery, and she's afraid of knives. Yet, here she is asleep and she can't stop you from seeing the damage age alone hasn't done, stop you from seeing what you've done, what you've both done. She can't cover it up. She can't save face. Those lines and creases and crow's feet are crowds of open mouths screaming you bastard, this is your fault, this is all your fault. The years of it on her face, her pale, naked face, and in her lungs, pooling in her lungs and sucking everything else in with it. That sharp edge to her collarbone, and her neck so thin, so thin. And here on her hand and wrist, this purple-blue bruise from where they struggled to find a vein, purple-blue fading red-yellow as it trails down the tendon to her finger and under her wedding ring, no make-up can disguise it.

She looks dead.

Is this how she'll look dead?

The tall nurse who put an end to your snoring as a courtesy to your wife isn't the one to ask. The nurse's high eyes looking down on you say move your arm, please, and move your chair, please, I need to get my tallness next to the bed and do helpful nurse things. "Why don't you go home and get some rest," she says with a short smile, a kind smile, "the doctors will know more tomorrow. Don't worry, she's in good hands."

Tomorrow you come back, and tomorrow night, and the next morning, and that next night, and soon you've missed three days of work and made a blur of Saturday morning's errands, remembering you forgot one of the bags of groceries at the store only as the gas-station attendant hollered to you before you cut back into traffic *didn't-you-want-the-cap-back-on-your-tank-what's-your-hurry-man* . . .

What your hurry is, man, is that they've drained your wife's lungs this morning. The doctor with the saliva problem will later tell you, without making eye contact, "Her breathing ishn't fully what we'd like to she," before he knuckles dry his moist mouth corners and has to dash. "But it is better than it was," the redheaded nurse will reassure shortly after he's left the room as she smoothes the folds in the plastic tenting. Meanwhile, park your ass in the car to finish as many of the must-do's as you have patience for, and after, "when?" "this afternoon," "when this afternoon?" you'll bring the boys to see her, touch her, "not too long in the room," you'll tell them in the elevator, "she'll be weak, but stronger," the tall nurse had said last night, just long enough to know Mummy's on the verge

of turning a corner, making progress, coming around, re-
covering nicely, on the mend, showing improvement, almost out of the woods they think, still, one very sick lady,
but she's a fighter, by Jupiter, she's a fighter, all and sundry
will have said at one time or another over the next several
weeks, though all you'll hear is buzz, buzz, buzz.

———•———

Only Adam, it turns out, is old enough to be allowed
in, old enough to have some of his senses allay some of
his fears.

"Ah, shvelbele," she says, weak, nasal, her words
wrapped in plastic. Two delicate fingers on the hand of
her tethered arm scissor-kick hello.

He approaches her bed in click with the oxygen.
"Mummy," he's excited, reaching for her.

"Careful of the tubes," she barely gets out.

"I know," his hand draws back quick, and quiet: "I
am, I am." And he is, he always is.

Anticipated pain averted, she sighs and her chest
drops. And "uh," she moans with flickering eyes. Hell
of hells is the spot below her breast, the nick between
ribs where they inserted the catheter to Roto-Rooter
her lungs.

No matter how sick, it's automatic. Love at arm's length, Myrmy, and who aches more.

Adam doesn't even need to shake his head; I know how his heart rationalizes. His bunched smile to me says Mummy is Mummy. You can tell time by her.

———

Out in the waiting room, too young to have their fears eased firsthand, Charlie and Josh look half their ages and twice them at the same time. Boys they are, hunched like gargoyles in orange chairs in a corner behind a philodendron, arms around knees, knees up to their chins, chins supporting scowls. But it's men's eyes, my eyes, narrowed and on fire, mad at who knows whom, me most, I figure, that glare at ads in *Life* and *Look* instead of at me.

"Why can't we see her now?"

"Because."

"But why?"

"Because."

"But why?"

"Be-cause."

Arguing with hospital protocol once again wouldn't get me their eyes. Assuring them that the doctors will make an exception "next time" isn't enough to comfort them, and when I try to cup their chins they yank their heads out of reach.

Even though.

Josh won't go to his mother with a cut finger. He'll wait for the all's-clear when he can come to me in secret and not have to apologize as he would to her for snagging his pinkie on broken glass, for digging in the dirt for arrowheads, for being a boy being a boy. I want to say to him look at me, I, too, am the Sun, not an emergency flashlight, not some space heater, but the Sun in all its intensity. I'm your father, Goddamnit, and I love you just as much and I can be the Sun all the time for you, too. Yet, in his universe, there is only one, and she's it. For Charlie, too, even with the way she rides him for the baby fat that's turned to boy fat, she's the warmth and glare for which there is no substitute.

Mummy's getting stronger, I try to say to them strong myself, Mummy's getting stronger, Mummy's getting better, everything's going to be back to normal, you'll see, better than normal, you'll see, Mummy will be home soon, and she's going to stay home from now on. But I stop short of saying Mummy's going to live and so am I.

Rules and regulations mean nothing to boys who want to see their mom now. Explanations and assurances mean nothing to boys who want to see their mom now. They see her closed door and they see me, and back they go to glaring at *Look* and at *Life* with my eyes. And like her lined face speaking for her, their sulking ones say you bastard, this is your fault, this is all your fault.

Crescent moon rising outside behind trees just starting to turn and back into your wife's room you go as if on autopilot. There's Adam against the window, a comfort to his mother from a safe distance, twilight on his back as he watches her sleep. I offer him the only smile I have left in me at the moment. He returns it in half, and I sit down heavy like it's the first time all day.

———

What must it be like to be weightless? To not feel fat legs in a white bubble suit, fat stomach, fat heart, as you float sparrow light, giving gravity the heave-ho? Does a bald head feel bald if no breeze blows across it, scalp soft as the Milky Way and helium for hair? Or, is it in Heaven as it is on Earth, Kingdom Come—backwards and all the prayers just talk? God?

———

"Yesh, hello? What? Oh. One moment, pleashe," the voice over the phone says to me, and I'm relieved that it's Dr. Phillips calling me back and not some late-night surprise. There's a rustling on his end that could be papers, could be him reciting the Lord's Prayer, it's hard to distinguish.

"Thanksh for holding." He's back. "Douglash Phillipsh here. Don?

"Dan."

"Dan? Dan. Da-a-a-n," he says, over a scratch rustle. "That'sh right. Sho. My shervice shaid you called?"

"Yesh," I say, "yes."

He clears his throat. "About?"

"About my boys getting in to see their mother?"

"Uh-huh?"

"You were going to leave orders at the nurse's station tonight that they'd be allowed in?"

"Uh-huh?"

"We got there and the nurse said you'd left no orders?"

"Uh-huh?"

"Well, did you or did you not leave orders? She said there were none, and once again, my boys couldn't see their mother. It's been over a month."

"Musht have been a shlipup, Don."

"Dan."

"Dan, of courshe. Ash I shaid, a shlipup, shurely. I inshtructed the nurshe's shtation on roundsh thish afternoon."

"The nurse said if it were up to her, the boys would be allowed in no problem. But she said she couldn't take that risk without authorization from the hospital or from you. Now, I'm getting sick and tired of this. My boys want to see their mother and Goddamnit so does she. I mean really, I could just spit."

"You don't shay."

"Look . . ."

"Temper, temper. I'm a doctor, not a shecretary.

"I realize that."

"And a very bishy doctor."

"I'm aware of that."

"And if I leave inshtructionsh and they're not carried out, what can I do?"

"You can leave them again. And make sure they're entered in her chart or whatever."

"Who'she the doctor here?"

"Oh, don't give me that."

"Lishen, lishen, we got off to a bad shtart here and it'sh probably my fault." He takes a dry pause. " I had to deliver a shpeech thish evening and, well, shuffishe it to shay, you can jusht imagine, I'm sure." He gurgles, and I feel my cheeks flush with shame. "That shaid; I under-shtand your frushtration, I do. But I have good newsh."

"Oh?"

"Yesh, very good newsh. Thoshe new filmsh we took? Exshellent. No fluidsh, no inflammation. Shcarring, yesh, but that'sh to be exshpected."

"So what are you saying?"

"What I'm shaying ish I don't she any reashon why she shouldn't go home shortly. Day after tomorrow even? Home for Halloween? Nishe treat for your boysh, don't you think? Her blood work looksh good, breathing ish good. No mucush to shpeek of, lucky lady."

"She doesn't seem herself."

"She's been through the wringer."

"And the fatigue?"

"She's going to have to take it very eashy for quite shome time, but I think given how far we've come she'll be much more comfortable at home from thish point on."

"She'll be normal?"

"Yesh."

"Her own self?"

"Yesh."

"Golly, that would be, that would be wonderful."

"I'll leave the ordersh tomorrow then. Don't worry, theshe ordersh will make it into her chart."

Blood flows into parts of my body that ceased up weeks ago. 3-IN-ONE Oil on rusted hinges this call is.

"Thank you, thank you, Doctor."

"My pleasure, Dean."

"Adam? Charlie? Josh? Mummy'sh coming home Wednesday," I hear myself yell even before hanging up the kitchen extension. "She'll be home for Halloween. Boys?" And then I remember it's past their bedtime and I've probably woken them. It's just as well. You take your good news where you can get it.

———

More leaves on the ground than on the trees, the golds and oranges she loves have curdled and there's been no apple outing this autumn, but she's home.

In bed, on her side of the bed, the mattress searching her thinned body for familiar curves.

Josh and Charlie curled in smiles on my side of the bed, careful as eggs around her, yet watch them slyly sliding knees and elbows closer and closer to just shy of touching.

Head of the pecking order is Adam at the foot of her, one hip tentative on the mattress, one leg at attention on the floor, ready to run for juice or tea or whatever her heart desires.

She smiles more than she sighs, and pale as she was when the orderly wheelchaired her to the car in the afternoon light, her skin has a skim coat of the orange wall's glow to it.

The boys soak her in: "How do you feel?" And "your hair's so long." And "you want to see Dusty Evsky's kittens?" And "Nana called." And "can I go trick or treating with Conan?" And "she said she'd call back when she thinks you're awake." And "she doesn't want us to wake you if you're not." And "can I?" And "do you want some juice?" And "cool, is that where the needle was?" And "Reverend Barker and Manny are moving." And "are you coming to the firehouse for the costume contest?" And "well?" And "go get your costume to show Mummy, Josh." And "what stain? It's just mustard, I don't know." And "do you still feel sick?" And "yeah, I did my homework at school." And "when are you going to be all better?" And "that's probably Nana calling back." And "hi, Nana." And "here." And "shh."

—·—

I could tell you a fable about a man who isn't me. Have him hosting a Saturday-night cocktail party in honor of his wife who was sick, but now's better, for friends who are more his than hers. With every rouged cheek kissed at the front door, he tosses an approving wink to the husband who beams beside her, and he pumps those husbands' hands as vigorously as a man among men does. "Good to see ya," he says. He takes their coats, their scarves, their hats at the door, doesn't look at any one item, hands the bulk to his wife behind him as he says about her "doesn't she look good as new?" (She'll separate the tangles scarf-by-arm and fit them best she can in the closet, careful of his custom-made camel's hair and the brand-new vicuna he bought himself while she was away.) "Let's get you warmed up, doll, shall we?" he says as he leads Gene's or Phil's or Arthur's wife to the bar, his hand on the small of whoever's back it is, and over his shoulder to the man whose wife she is, adds, "scotch rocks, sport, right?" There's a fire burning. Licking and hissing as spontaneously as his guests. The hearth of his home—his deed, his sweat—he takes care of his family and every man there knows it. He stands before the flames collar-open, elbow on mantel, his prize Boxer bitch at his feet, her docked ears prick stiff by her master's side. Platters of food replenish, ashtrays overflow and empty, he catches the moonlight in Phil's wife's eye, she's a looker, and with things in his world so silky all a man in his own element need do now is pitch another log on the fire.

There are men whose children buy them neckties for Father's Day. There are men whose wives know the Saturday-night signal. Goddamn them.

———

Day by day, in doses, she's up, dressed down in cardigans and skirts too long for the fashion she'd be in fashion in, hair longer than she'd ever allowed, not smoking, not working, the pace of her hardly the same woman who used to gallop Grand Central in heels. Home when the boys leave for school and when they return. Home with the car and keys while I hitch rides to and from the station in the dark. Home cleaning out cupboards with Ingerlil, cleaning out closets, cleaning out drawers, letting the dogs out, letting the dogs in, knitting with unvarnished fingers, reading, breathing clear, staying warm, happy, she says, being the kind of woman the kind of man she wanted wants.

But that kind of woman isn't the kind of woman she is, and all of us know it. This life here in the woods is a nice dream, a habitable landscape, but there's not enough oxygen to keep all the parts of her pumping blood forever. Weeknights dusk to dawn, Friday night Sabbath to sundown Sunday she makes a good show of it. Yet turn on the television and a clever advertising slogan she wasn't there to write yields a sigh and tight eyes and a shake of the head, and I know her restless hands miss the cigarettes they used to hold, and the typewriter keys, and the office memos, and the restaurant napkins, and the train tickets, and the charge-a-plates.

———

Winter snows give way to crocuses on the hill where the boys race sleds and living on my salary alone after six months doesn't do it. Having no truck tracks score the driveway since UPS stopped delivering doesn't do it. A housekeeper-less back bedroom since Ingerlil met an oncologist in the city and became his second wife doesn't do it. Meat loafs dry as adobe and dog hair everywhere and laundry that needs refolding after the boys have done it doesn't do it.

Mummy's become any old Mom in the woods and "neat" and "cool" aren't the words the boys use anymore about their exotic bird, or about having their exotic bird home. "Isn't this nice," and "aren't you glad I'm here," are coming less often from her lips, and like the Day-Glo bright lipstick on her otherwise unmade-up face, the questions sound otherworldly. The novelty has started

to wear thin for them as well as her, annoying and repetitive and thin as the spring parkas she's home to
hound them to wear on days they needn't, annoying and
repetitive and thin as each "because I said so."

She's the monolith in *2001*, sleek and tall and out
of place among the apes, fixed in the ground and going
nowhere, screeching her high-frequency screech.

———

It's a far cry from the quiet grief of Mary Fence. With
Ed dead, her days are small as nesting boxes, her only
forays out her afternoon pilgrimage to the mailbox at the
end of the lane, where she and Myrmy sometimes force
their heads high to chat like any other neighbors in the
woods, and her weekly drive to the liquor store where
she spends what's left of Ed's monthly Social Security
and Veteran's benefits. Her daughters look more like
hippies everyday, Myrmy says, the older ones running
wild, glassy-eyed in the passenger seats of Volkswagens,
laughing a little too loud as their boyfriends navigate
the unpaved lane at speeds too fast for the ruts. The
boyfriends' hair long as Mary's daughers', Myrmy says,
blowing in their eyes and out the open windows and
Mary doesn't see it, Myrmy says, because she's only

looking in her glass. And Myrmy says, in a voice I think only women can truly hear, "and who can blame her."

I doubt Mary's the kind of widow she ever thought she'd be, if she ever even gandered into the future that far, much less the kind of widow the kind of man she wanted wanted before he became the kind of man he became, Ed. All his smoky, liquory, rail-thin dying in plain sight negligence. Jesus, Ed, Jesus, how could you do it? How could you let it happen? You let it happen, my friend, you let it happen and your wife isn't strong enough to carry on without you. Mary isn't Myrmy, or the Myrmy Myrmy was before she got sick. You let it happen, my friend, and I couldn't stand watching it unfold in you like the war on the nightly news. Do you understand why I backed away from you these last years? You in your smoky, liquory, rail-thin, full-head-of-hair tallness, you were me in a parallel universe, me in a fun-house mirror. You've been dead a year and it doesn't feel any more merciful now than it did then that you are, the legacy of your negligence goes on as far as the eye can see.

———

The important things said between husbands and wives aren't said in words. Sighs, and sounds from cups placed too hard on saucers, zippers ripping like plows, the dogs' names barked, 250 pounds hitting the floor are like radio transmissions, all snaps and pops and fizzles full of invective, conveying what words can't. It's not the music we thought we'd hear coming through the trees fourteen years ago, but it is what came to us and it is what stuck in our heads and my only hope is that the boys are able to get the tune out of theirs and not wake to it for the rest of their lives.

———

Standing in front of the toilet, dick in hand, peeing into the bowl, feeling the blood draining from my head as if it were in the heavy stream, either I pitched forward and caught the windowsill, or my shoulder led left to clip the handle of the shower door, one or the other I don't know, the piss on the floor and on my pants leg, the shattered lens of my glasses, the blood in the shards, the deep gash above my left eye are the only clues I have to go on that some kind of countdown occurred and at one I passed out and fell.

———

As the emergency-room doctor digs the needle across the gash and trusses it like a stuffed chicken, one stitch two stitch three stitch four, all I can think about is that my wife didn't die, close as she came, and strong as she is again she just may be the first person ever who doesn't.

————

"You have to go back to work," I say to her in the car as she drives us home.

"I know," she says, just making the yellow as it's turning red. "I was just thinking the same thing."

————

Up they went in a towering cone and down they've plunked in a sharp-edged box. If God was along for the ride he didn't say much, but I suspect He jumped out first like a little kid, like he'd been there all this time, just waiting for his friends to arrive. First feet on ground that knows nothing about nothing except the minerals at its core; no wars, no illness, no sadness of a human kind, at least. Joy. Just joy. Cool, glowing, million-mile-away joy. Where anything is possible. And every day the beginning.

NINE

Drive.

"TEACH ME TO DRIVE," I SAID WHERE THE HENRY Hudson hands the reins to the Saw Mill River. We were in the convertible, the green and tan Buick Special, borrowed from the very same roommate I'd canceled on when Dan's come-on caught my breath. Al, his name was, Al Morris, a Captain then, a Colonel now, whom I threw over sight unseen, and good thing, too, for the girl I later fixed him up with, Adele Steinbrecher, never did learn to drive, not that Buick, nor any car after. Al sits in the passenger seat for no one 'cept his staff sergeant driver to this day, Adele's crowed with wifely pride to us more than once, crowed in tidy letters from their far-flung foreign postings, letters that often spout about their dogs Nash and Edsel as if they were children. Even after that goyishe wedding of theirs at the Cloisters, champagne and strawberries like it was Oyster Bay and nary a Jew without an assimilated name or nose among the guests, and Al boasting to his army buddies "I'd do anything for this little gal." Yet here it is near seventeen years later and he has yet to do more for her than a little diamond spray and a summer shack by the shore.

"Teach me to drive," I said, the top down and my new short hair barely rippling in the breeze, but the nip for late June, sunny as it was, wasn't forecast and the cashmere car coat wasn't excessive as Dan ribbed. No argument, no delay, he pulled us over to a parking strip, empty but for a copper sedan bulbous as an unpeeled onion. At the wheel, a sullen young man flapping a map as far as possible from the young woman at his side, and the young woman at his side, staring blank as we passed, sitting useless as the Venus de Milo. He pulled past them and parked us in the shade from a copse of lush beeches. They were so slinky tall and well mannered, those trees, they could have been shopgirls fanning out a gown's ample yardage the way the branches chiffoned. He didn't even turn off the engine. Shifted into park and opened his door and leaned into me and kissed me all one movement. Left a trace of lime after-shave on my cheek and not a rough hair from his close razoring, kissed me and said deep down "anything ya want" and winked and stayed close and I couldn't take my eyes off his naughty-boy smile. How handsome he looked in that shade, dappled dark and all ruddy, his hair receding only just, and what an idiot his ex-wife must have been. He climbed out not a groan, and I slid over giddy, pulled my skirt like it was a little red wagon onto the spot where the heat of him still lingered. In the mirror, my lipstick held its own, SundayRed, too strong for church but perfect for lay activities, as he settled in beside me and made me a headrest of his arm.

"Ya know which is the brake and which is the gas, right?" he smiled and rolled his eyes for me. That much I knew, who doesn't know that much, except maybe Adele, still, much as she'd enjoy the waspy name, though maybe not the room-for-a-family-of-five-plus-dogs-ness of our new car, a Country Squire. "There's not much to it," his smile continued, "just shift her into D and ease us back on the road. Don't worry," he said, his voice smoothing the nerves in my face, "I'm right here and I won't let anything happen."

"Teach me to drive," I said, and he did, no argument, no delay, matter-of-fact as a reflex, as if he was expecting the day to come, looking forward to it like a parent with a child steps from walking. Imagine me an Adele married to an Al and no driver's license, or a Howard and no résumé. Imagine the likes of either of them taking to the passenger seat as enthusiastically as the likes of Dan did, settling in for the drive while I learned on the fly. Any jitters I had flattened when that roar vibrated through my pump as I pressed the pedal, came right through it and shinnied up my calf and thigh and I'm making something so big move the way I want it to and he saw that on my face and smiled wide and no wonder men love cars.

The likes of none other would have taught me how to keep pace with them, keep pace and then accelerate past, without ever lording it over, never once, not like I would, like I have, lorded that I wouldn't have learned without him, and who's to say that without him I would have.

———·———

A new job at twice my former pay; a new wardrobe for summer and I'm treating myself to a mink this fall; the new station wagon navy blue and paneled and big as Connecticut that I picked out and paid for; Delphine, the new girl, *je suis enceinte de six mois, madame* she con-

fessed last week when I caught her eating cold canned
turtle soup, and next week her husband comes from
Haiti to take her home to their other five, that took
some finagling; someone named Felice, single, I made
sure, queued up to take her place, for ten minutes or so;
Charlie and Josh at a new summer camp, Charlie hating
how the uniforms pinch and Josh's poison-pen letters
letting us know he hates everything else; Adam cleaning offices and learning Greek for the summer; they do
grow so fast; a very odd man with a grumpy accent and
a Jaguar that Dan envies and a much younger wife in
Reverend Barker's old house; Dusty Evsky's kittens having kittens; Dan's Dan; and me, hale as if I'd never been
sick a day in my life I tell Adele in a tidy letter back.

As I lick the envelope there's the green and tan chair
in the playroom that's full of Dan, my never a Colonel
and not much left of the Captain, half asleep in front
of a program he half slept through last fall, and I say:
"Dan, you're going to a doctor, I don't care what you say,
they've landed on the moon, who knows what else is
possible, you're going."

Come through an illness on the other side and you
want everyone around you to feel it, Goddamnit, like
love.

He says "and do what, what are they going to do?"

I'm so glad we had this time together.

And I say, not angry, not a twitch in my jaw, like the answer's been there calm all the time, neat and simple, "something."

And he says "something? Huh. I see. Some thing."

Just to have a laugh or sing a song.

And I say "yes, some thing. How should I know? They were able to do it to you; maybe now they can undo it. You don't know. Some thing. You have to try. We have to find some one."

Seems we just get started and before you know it.

"Where," he says. "Where are we going to find some one?"

And I say "some where. We'll find some one, some where. Some one some where must be able to do some thing."

Comes the time we have to say so-long.

"Dan."

And his lumbering eyes snap to, and he tugs his ear-lobe, *Good night, everybody,* and groans as he hoists his weight from the chair and throws it at the television to change the channel. *Another amazing day for the amazing Mets.* His face in profile for that split second glowing Etch-A-Sketch gray shows nothing of the man who beamed his high beams at me. *Stay tuned for* The Late Show *and tonight's feature, The Attack of the Fifty-Foot Woman.* Battery low, he's all flat tires and broken taillights backing to the chair, falling into the chair, the chair that's always there for him like a garage.

"I'll find someone. You'll see."

Fast relief with Phillips' Milk of Magnesia.

Just below the one nostril there are hairs his razor missed, I think. He doesn't even blink when I strike strike strike the match for my cigarette.

And then, changing channels myself.

"What do you think about taking the boys to Europe next summer? Dan."

"Hmm?"

"Next summer. Europe. We take the boys. They should go."

Last night I dreamed I went dancing in my Maidenform Bra.

He's awake now, some part of him at least.

"Are you crazy? They'll be wanting hamburgers all the time."

"I'm going to start a trip fund anyway."

"You do that."

"I want us to go."

"Whatever you want."

"I'm going to," I say to my cigarette.

"Jesus, Myrmy, enough."

And my brand speaks back from the TV: *Come alive with pleasure.*

———

Am I going too fast, or have I hit the speed at which I was meant to travel?

———

Come through an illness on the other side and the life that's always been is still there, still needing attending to, coordinating, scheduling, driving, pushing, paying for, bending over backwards for, living, because that is what it is about. I'll be damned if I was lying fallow all those months only to come out the other side back at square one, further back, outside the hopscotch completely, with nothing up ahead but more of the same, or worse.

That I could stay in the woods, be Mommy, give up the train and the city and the stores and the money and the words, above everything else the words, everything that keeps me from withering on the vine, and have Dan stay Dan? Insanity.

Hard as he tried, and he tried, he did try to keep things going, make the sun rise and set without incident, buoy the boys' spirits and mine, be strong for us all, provide for us all when he barely has enough in him to float alone: it wasn't enough, not nearly.

Falling asleep mid-sentence, at the table, behind the wheel; this is not someone who can keep things going, keep things going, alone.

How small he must have felt, small in the eyes of his sons, small after last summer's scene in the Morrises' driveway when he ordered his sons to call him Sir. Lining them up as he did like new recruits under the Labor Day sun, dog faces in need of strict training, and chewing them out for embarrassing him in front of his still-active army buddy. It was only sunburns and swimming fatigue and back-to-school anxieties coming out of the corners of their mouths. Yet there on that gravel outside of that cottage in front of that friend it was sass to his reddened ears, sass like no enlisted man would dare do to Colonel Al. He commanded them to address him as Sir. He exhumed the army in him and flicked off the mothballs and commanded his sons to call their daddy Sir. He expected them to get behind the wheel of it, no training, no practice run, release the parking brake and shift to S and call him Sir. And they did. They hung their heads and mumbled it, in triplicate: Sir. They wanted to please him. They saw it in the tears on my cheek that they should. But it had no meaning, and he knew it. They knew it, we all knew it. Under that hot, late sun how much it mattered to him in front of that friend to shiver to life a mirage of the fit Sir he used to be. The fit Sir I spurned his buddy for and married. Never mind that he had sired sons, fired nothing but "silver bullets" Al said after Josh was born, fathering son after son after son for a life more intimate than any army barracks could provide. But to him in that moment, being Daddy wasn't enough, not nearly. In front of that friend who only had strangers to call Son, he wanted to be the Sir he hadn't been for years, the Sir his sons have only ever known as Daddy. And when it mattered even more, when being Daddy really mattered, mattered most to the rest of us, Daddy wasn't enough, again.

Sir or Daddy, Mommy or Myrmy; do any of us ever really measure up in the moments that matter most? Can any of us ever forgive ourselves for the two halves that never quite come whole? Or must we atone for the rest of our lives for the people we don't have it in us to be?

Shame of shames, no one deserves to see themselves as they cannot be. To see me come out the other side of almost dead, new and improved, a Phoenix with not a dusting of ash on my wings up and aloft and flapping my miles a minute, miles ahead of his best, soaring high as ever and always landing, Neil Armstrong to his Iccarus, what a slap.

"Teach me to drive," I said, and you did, no argument, no delay, matter-of-fact as a reflex and what did I do to you in return? Oh Captain, my Captain, did I stop you from becoming the Colonel you might have been, the kind of man whose sons call him Sir and say it with admiration? The kind of man whose wife crows about his every conceit and means it with all her heart?

Splash your cares away with Jean Naté.

Oh Captain, my Captain, let me give you back your life.

Let me drive this one last time.

Let me give you next year, and the year after that, and the year after that, and the years after that.

"I'll call Phillips. He'll know shomeone," I say to his head as it falls to his chest. Say it as the woman in the

TV movie runs from her husband and their car, runs up to the big moon figure that's blocking their road, runs up to it and pounds her fists on it, yelling *No! No! No!*

It's the least I can do.

————

Come home late from a later train to find Josh and Charlie in the driveway at dusk, flickers of chrome in the headlights as they bicycle around the turnaround, circle after circle in opposite directions.

Swing right over the sinkhole that looks to me to be growing bigger than what Dan claims a simple patch job will patch, skid a bit on the loose gravel coming up through the tar and the wet leaves the boys were supposed to rake, "careful," he says and I ignore it, scrape something on the hump, the muffler, "are you listening" gets my best arched brow, nose the car to the garage door as always and both of us bump a bit when I stop hard.

Dusk getting darker and there the two of them still are, not enough on and sweating in the chill, circling the new stone planter in the circle, one going this way, one going that, in the shadows they could be bats. Tilt their heads up to us as if by accident, lackluster "oh, hi" leapfrogs an "oh, hey" as we're half out the car doors, look at each other as their paths cross exchanging something I know not what but something.

I say: "what's doing? How are you? Where's Adam?"

Josh circles and trails a shoulder-shrugged "mm-mm-mm."

Dan says to me: "did you put the parking brake on" and I just look at him.

Something's not right so I say: "Charlie?"

And aiming at a cat: "uh-huh?"

"Is Adam inside," Dan says instead of me saying it and he looks at me like I'm supposed to be clairvoyant. The boys circle another circle and exchange another look and Dan's cheek pulses just a bit where his bridge doesn't quite fit, and he says "OK," in the mad voice I haven't heard for about a month, "what's going on?"

It's Josh who jerks to a stop on the far side of the planter, foot against a loose stone, a crunch, stares down to confirm that yes, there in the dark, that was new cement already crumbling out. He bounces his behind on the banana seat as Charlie circles past him; and, looking past me to Dan on his way to ruining a rhododendron it's Charlie who says: "ask Adam."

Nobody's bothered to turn on the light to the back

door, let alone the driveway. "My head is already splitting," I say and Dan hmphs.

Inside, life as we know it not at all how I want it.

"Adam" I call out in the dark kitchen, the dark dining room, the dark playroom, never mind the dark living room, and I can't tell if he answers or not from down the hall from where there's a glow under his door because Aggie and Jazzbo are at me, snarfling and jumping and slobbering and wagging their stubs, toenails clicking on the linoleum, and their collar chains and tags jangling right to my left lobe and dammit that's saliva on my mink. "Away."

"Move," Dan says behind me and that jab better be the box from his shirts and not one of the hangers from the dry cleaning.

"Wait," I say, "wait, will you? Let me get the light for crying out loud." The storm door slams behind him and I can't see the look on his face but right now I don't want to. "Adam."

His "I'm, um, coming" coming from the hallway has that same hesitant tone to it that he uses when telling us to expect, pause, an A- among his ninety-two A's on his report card.

"Where's Felice," I say. "What's going on," I say.

"Where is she," Dan says. "And dinner?"

"And dinner." That's right. "Where is dinner?"

"Um."

"Is this Thursday?"

"No," Dan says. "Tuesday."

"Actually, it's Wednesday," Adam says, and then says: "Don't get upset," he says, and that's all the cue my right lobe needs to join the drumming.

I say, trying not to grind my teeth: "where is she?"

And Adam says, after a pause: "she, um, she quit."

And Dan says: "she quit?"

And Adam pauses another um.

And I say, putting down the anvil that is my pocket-book: "what did she say?"

And he ums and says: "not much. Just that she quits and um."

"And what," I say.

And he says: "um, she just said that, um, well, that's all she said, she didn't say."

"Why didn't you call one of us," I say, adjusting the shoulder that doesn't feel any better bag off or not.

And Adam says: "um, I didn't want to upset you at work."

And Dan says, "how did she leave here?"

And Adam says: "um, a cop picked her up," and he shrugs.

And Dan says: "a skinny one?"

And Adam says: "like Ichabod Crane."

What are they talking about? I have to hang my coat up and get some aspirin and now we have to start with dinner, I realize. "We have to start with dinner now?"

And Dan says: "I'll do it."

And I say: "it's chickens. Two chickens. It'll be hours before we can eat." And Adam's about to um again when I realize: "if they're defrosted."

And he gets in another um and I swear they don't um in Latin, unless it's at the end of a sentence at the end of a verb and he gets A's in Latin so why is Adam um-ing so much and he ums again and says: "she took 'em."

"The chickens," Dan says. "She took the chickens?"

I'm thinking she took the chickens? And say: "she took the chickens?"

And Dan says to me, "what did you say to her?"

"She took dinner," I say to Adam.

"Right from the freezer," he says to Dan.

And Dan says to me, "did you say something to her about the thing?"

I don't care that she's gone, good riddance, I say, but she took my chickens, how do you like that.

"How do you like that," Dan says to me as I open the freezer and sure enough: no chickens. "You said something, didn't you?"

"I'm hungry," Charlie says from the kitchen door.

"I told her from now on she could walk to church, like Christ."

And Dan says, "if she can walk, you can cook. It's a miracle. Guess she told you."

"Can we go to Howard Johnson's," Josh says from behind Charlie, "for fried clams?"

"I can't start with this all over again," I say to Dan.

"With what," he says.

The storm door slams once more as the other two come in.

"Don't slam the door, my head. With this housekeeper nonsense."

"You should have thought of that before," he says, dropping the shirt boxes on the dining table, which knocks over the rooster salt shaker.

"Watch what you're doing," I say and I don't say anything more.

After a moment, after a sigh, the deep kind you hear in movies that you can't believe are real, but they are, because people really do do them in real life when there's nothing else to do but sigh deep instead of giving in to the overwhelming urge to scream, Dan sighs and says: "so we won't get another."

His face so flushed. Because his coat's still on?

And I say, a little less mad because of his coloring: "no?"

And he says: "no."

He'd loosen his tie if it weren't already loosened. He doesn't look like he's getting enough air.

So I say: "so what are we supposed to do?"

And he says: "the sky's not going to fall down if we don't have a housekeeper. They're not babies anymore. They don't need one."

And I say: "what about meals?"

And he says: "they can get their own breakfasts and I'll make their lunches at night or they can buy them. And I'll fix dinner."

"You'll get off the train every night and start with dinner?"

"Yes."

"You will."

"Yes."

"And clean up after?"

"They can do that."

Charlie and Josh groan in unison and look at Adam.

They know "they" means the two of them only, not him. His homework comes first. He doesn't look back.

"And the laundry, too," I say.

"It'll get done," he says. What he means is: don't say anything more.

Don't tell me not to say anything more. "Because I'm not going to," I say, saying more, "I'm telling you that right now," I say, "I'm exhausted enough," I say, and I mean it. "I'm not doing all of that and all the driving. Because of that girl. I'm sorry. I am not."

Dan looks down at his shoes. There's not much shine left on them so he can't see me.

Adam jumps between us, um-less. "I can help with the driving," he says. "I'll have my license in two weeks."

"Yeah," Charlie says, half Dan mad, half me, "but what about dinner tonight?"

He kicks the door, which startles the dogs, which jangles their chains, which goes straight to my eye sockets.

My head feels like it's being pounded on. By two frozen chickens.

—·—

Two weeks, Adam said. Two weeks. Can it already be a year since I got sick? Come full circle and punch the inside out, now it's me driving and driving and driving and driving and driving and driving because Dan can't.

A month ago he got stopped for speeding, his third ticket in a year. One more said the cop and they'd take his license away. "They always say that," he said to me when I said to him and I couldn't believe I was saying it "you better slow down," and he said back "mind your own business."

He'd been out looking at empty storefronts, empty storefronts in which to open a restaurant. The idea isn't new; he's had it in the back of his mind for years now. Way back in the back of his mind, in the attic in an envelope in a suitcase behind a trunk, hidden as far back as my own desire to write lyrics, and I've held no more store in him opening a restaurant than me opening on Broadway. But no skin off my nose, let him dream, let him look, what could it hurt, he's a good cook, God knows his silhouette is advertising enough, he wouldn't have to commute, I'd rather he had a partner but I'm staying out of it until it gets to that point, we'll see.

So he was out looking at empty storefronts, "scouting," he called it. Scouting in Eastport, Fairport, Norport, searching Highport and Lowport as if it was suddenly

a matter of the utmost import, and someplace between
Toport and Froport the sirens, the ticket, the report.

Bad enough.

Two weeks later, two weeks ago, that girl, that Felice,
that chicken thief got it in her head that she just had to
go to church. Hadn't gone a single Sunday in the month
she'd been here, but all of a sudden she got "the call" like
it was issued ex cathedra. "Meester," she begged Dan,
"Meester, please drive me church, oh please." Begged
him at dawn, before he'd had his coffee I'm guessing,
certainly before I was awake, because I would have said
to her "you can go to ten o'clock mass with Mrs. Fence
down the lane," but no, she got "the call" and "the call"
was strong and "the call" said six o'clock mass and it said
it at ten till. So he took her. And he sped. And hiding
behind a fence on Whippoorwill Lane was the cop car
and they stopped him like he was trying to cross the
border into Switzerland. And like the other cop warned
him, they took away his license then and there. One
cop drove him home in the car, another cop, scrawny,
I gather, followed after dropping Bernadette-of-the-
Woods at the church. I had just pried myself out of
bed, shivering with a first frost and the furnace not yet
going, up and no one in the kitchen and I look out the

front window and all I see is the cop car going down
the hill and that warmed me right up and then I hear
Dan climbing the garage steps. Heavy steps, his heaviest
steps, his madder-than-hell heavy steps. And I knew, I
just knew, somehow I just knew what had happened. I
didn't even need to say "I told you so" when he varfed
through the door just like the boys do when I tell them
to come in when they don't want to come in, because
the red in his face said he'd heard me say it even before
I'd said it and I hadn't even said it and before I was even
tempted to say it just to say it he said "don't say it" so
instead I said "so now what, speedy?"

Three months without his license. He'll have it back
some time around New Year's. "Teach me to drive," I
said all those years ago and good thing, too.

———•———

Phone calls from the office, one after another after another every other day, lose an earring taking it off and
on and off and on and off to hold the receiver to my
ear, and trying to type with it on my shoulder, operator,
what was that number, hello, hello, break a nail dialing, Goddamnit, call back Phillips's nurse, did he say
Shepshy and mean Sepsy, can't find a Sepsy there's no

Sepsy, Shepshy, really, you're sure, call Sloan-Kettering, call Columbia Presbyterian, call Mount Sinai, Jews always know, Shepshy: no, referred to Loedeke: no, what about in Boston, St. Louis, Minneapolis, Bethuin at the Mayo says doing things with radiation and thyroids in Chicago, someone named Lipp or Lapp or Lepp, no Rush, Rush in Chicago, Rush in Chicago, Rush in Chicago. Rush? Spell that.

Phone calls to Rush in Chicago, one after another after another every other day, he's in conference, he's at a conference, he's in surgery, he's out sick, he'll be back after Thanksgiving, call back next Tuesday, he'll have to call you back next Friday, back from lunch and Hannukah shopping, Rush from Chicago returned your call, return his call, he's gone for the day, did he get my letter, he's eager to talk to you, will he be there in the morning, will you be there in the afternoon, Dr. Rush well how do you like that I was beginning to think you were a ghost. It's my husband, Dan.

———

Pickwickian syndrome, Rush said.

He repeated it for me. Pickwickian syndrome.

It could be that, he said.

An advanced form of narcolepsy. A rare form. We don't see it that often, he said, but it's a fascinating turn in the road.

Especially a case like this, from what it sounds like, he said, where the thyroid has lost its compass completely. Leads to all sorts of complications: diabetes, heart disease, weight gain, he said. You say he's a large man, he said. It could be that, he said. Sounds to me like it could be that.

Radiation can do that to the thyroid, he said. It does other things, too, we're finding, things we never suspected, he said, but we'll go into that later.

Or, he said, pausing, and I stiffened in my chair listening to him inhale, it could be something else, he said. Up with his breath, my heart, and down again. We'll know more when we run tests, he said. We can't be certain of anything until we run tests.

Blood work, of course, and arterial traces, and tissue samples, he said.

CAT scans and EKGs and EEGs, he said.

And X rays.

Yes, he said, we'll have to do some X rays.

Pickwickian Syndrome. What a name. How Dickensian. So *Bleak House.* I am born.

I was trying to keep up with him, write it all down, even used the back of an ad rough as a notepad. On one side, two views of a woman's head. To the left, the before: a drab, mouse-colored, tangled mane you'd rather blind yourself than see mocking you in your mirror. On the right, the after: lustrous, salon-perfect chestnut tresses any mirror would fall over itself to reflect. Her secret? She did it herself. At home. With a three-step, total hair-care breakthrough in shiny manageability. Lucky girl. All she has to do is step in the shower and voilà: problems solved. The client loves this ad, spilled coffee on his ascot in the meeting he was so excited that I'd made shampoo sound scientific. A breakthrough. I'm getting a raise because of it.

———

We have a name attached to the unknown, maybe attached, I keep having to remind myself, but a name, a something, this thing, his thing, it has a name, maybe, maybe it has a name and I want to say it.

Pickwickian syndrome. I enunciate it under my breath to Mae Swoon at dinner, without the others hearing, Pauline and Phil and Mae's husband, Gene, and Dorothy and Walter and Dan, of course, the eight of us at the table, toasty warm if too tightly seated in oh-so-petite Café Somnoler, reservations two months in advance for New Year's Eve, I reminded Pauline to make them. Mae's face is crunching she's trying so hard to hear me whisper as we meet each other over the salt and pepper, but it's not working. "Pigwiggian, what?" she rasps back and dips her head nearer to mine, fingers her flip out of the way and her pearl clip-on is lipstick-close to my mouth for me to repeat, but Dan's looking at me cockeyed from behind Walter's graying bristles so I cover and say louder than necessary, "your earrings are darling."

The boys' faces weren't so complicated when I told them. No fighting the clinking of silverware on china, nor high school–age waiters in white jackets with hair to their shoulders explaining that yes ma'am the scallops are frozen, but the steak tartare is fresh, more champagne? There was no need to whisper to my own children in my own house at my own dining-room table in front of my own husband that I found a doctor from out-of-town who thinks he may know what Daddy's condition is and he's coming to meet with Daddy. Daddy will check into the hospital after New Year's, he'll check in on Sunday, the fourth is it, Dan? He'll check in, they'll do some tests, and he'll stay overnight and the doctor will arrive from Chicago the following day and meet with him and then we'll see, isn't that wonderful?

Smiles all around in proportion to their faith in the unknown and their understanding of the concrete. Josh's thin lips bite into the good news whole, the space between his front teeth out for the world to see. It's hard to tell if he truly comprehends, or if he's reading the relief on my face and simply mirroring me, or if it's that he's a ten-year-old being told good things will happen and he believes it because he has no reason not to. Looking from me to Dan and back he doesn't ask questions, none of them do, but his big smile and clear eyes say "yay" and that's good enough for now. Charlie's cheeks, if they weren't so fleshy, might stretch wider to let his lips part as full as they wish to and allow his perfect uppers and lowers to register his delight. From behind long bangs his eyes scan Dan's body as if they were seeing sickness rise off the flesh right there. His elbows rocking on the table speak to his impatience for good news to kick in, if not this minute perhaps in time for his Bar Mitzvah in February. Or might he be as tickled to stretch out Christmas vacation an extra week before school resumes? That, too; that Charlie boy, he makes his own timetables. Adam's smile is wide, yet not wide enough to show any teeth at all. He doesn't give himself over to good news outright; better it should be proven immutable with footnotes and a table of contents and a Library of Congress catalogue number. To him, good news you can go to sleep on isn't "you're sure to be cured," it's "you are." Even so, there is hope on his face, pleasure in his eyes, there's no mistaking it in his narrow shoulders relaxing into his chair back, the way his fine hands sit flat on the table not fidgeting, Adam wants the good news to be.

But Dan's smile is the least convinced of all. His sons beam all around him, they could be the glow on his bare head and you'd think he'd soak in their happiness, but his half-eyes are lowered to his plate and fixed on the stripped steak bone on it. Is he embarrassed? Skeptical? Asleep? Softer than normal I say "Dan," gift-wrapping his name with my voice and the nudging does the trick, moves the needle on the record and unsticks the song. His eyes climb over his glasses to take in our faces around the table. One by one, refilling our smiles with air, Adam to his right, then Josh, then across to me, then Charlie on his left. Then a second look I don't expect: back to me for a pause no longer than a blink. What's in that pause I'll never know. Then back to his plate his eyes go and he nods and tries to be more generous with his mouth, "we'll see," he says with his bottom lip flared, his head nodding and nodding, "we'll see."

At the office, I must be saying his name more than usual I guess. Another writer on the blander accounts, a girl I haven't had much to do with, much younger than me though not as bold even in her miniskirts, smart enough cookie, however, to handle dog kibble and drain openers, says to me in the ladies' room mirror, "a husband, sons, a house in the woods, looks, talent, a mink, you really have it all," and my eyeliner slips ever so to hear such a summary. Don't jinx it.

———

"Oh, cool," Josh says to Dan when he sees the car keys in his father's hand. "You got your license back? Hey, Mom." His whole gangly body is one with the surprise, chicken arms and bird legs nimble as he and Dan play catch with the keys. He doesn't even mind when Charlie bumps him silly to take his place in the game.

"OK, fellas," I say joining them at the door just as Adam does, "give us a kiss. Adam, you have the restaurant's number?" Of course, he nods. "And the Swoons', we should be there by ten. Don't stay up too late." I spare them my lipstick and offer each a cheek. Shvelbele, shvelbele, shvelbele. It's cold out, Dan, you want your scarf?"

"Be good," he says to them as I hand him my pocket-book so I can tie the belt around my coat. He holds the bag away from him like a dirty diaper, and as he leans in to kiss each on the forehead it near-misses their ribs. Adam Charlie Josh in order, oldest to youngest, tallest to shortest, good-night kisses all the same, lips to brows. He'd rather stay home with them than socialize in a jacket and tie, but he offers me back the bag as he has a thousand times, not even looking, and it means we're set, we're going. The keys jingle in his left hand, the doorknob clicks with his right and the cold blast that comes in when he pulls the door in and pushes the storm door out takes us all by surprise. We step onto the stoop, where the frost on the concrete glistens in the porch light, and he says back to the boys with a wink and a plume of steam, "we'll see you next year." Charlie bats his eyes psychedelic and har-hars, giving in to a he-he before he body rolls the front door closed. Dan palms an extra push on the storm door to make the broken latch catch.

—·—

The frost on the stoop is the frost on the car is the frost on the road is the frost on the windows at the restaurant, dimmed chandeliers and finger-thick tapers in silvers and maroons glowing crystal within. Frosted sand on the sliver of beach behind the restaurant, frost on the rocks of a sometime jetty, and all of Long Island Sound at low tide dressed in black.

Few patches of snow remain from the Christmas Eve storm that the weathermen so smugly insisted would be a dusting before they had to adjust their cufflinks and eat their words. Patches of it, crisped and dirty, outside a driveway here and there where the plows made their piles, swaths of it along side garages blown in on winds that blew away, and now and then a mailbox like the Swoons' knocked for a loop by a skid.

Gene said to him when the evening was still hors d'oeuvres, "so what's new, Danny boy," and Dan's response is still on my mind. "Oh, same old, same old."

"Why don't you want to tell anybody," I ask him on the drive home. The satin lining of my mink is a frozen scarlet, making me even colder while waiting for the heat to come on.

"Because." He says in his tired voice. "It's not anything yet." His tired tone somewhere between "did you set the alarm?" and "good night."

I try to keep my own voice awake but not too. "But it's good news, Dan. It's something to hope for."

"I know," he says.

It's not the bells and whistles I want to hear. "You know," I say, shaking my head, though not from shivering. "What, is it a burden to you?"

And fast, "of course, not," he says, and he looks over at me, his eyes off the road and over at me over his glasses. "Let's not get ahead of ourselves," he says. "OK? We'll see what happens." His tone is more awake than it was, reassuring, kindly, apologetic even, and his words make sense. As I turn to him to say that I hear that, know that, am OK with that for now, true or not, he's already turned his attention back to the road.

The road and the lights, the lights coming at us fast. He flashes his beams to make them lower theirs they stay he accelerates make them pass faster and the bright lights closer blind us brighter bright hitting white white the car's at us white my eyes bright honking kids yelling "happy new year's!" as they go by and they're gone, and dark again. Our beams on the frost only. Heat's on. Breathing. Calm. Quiet. Us. Alone on the road.

Eleven O'clock Hill. Lyon's Plains. River Bend.

Husband at the wheel and wife at his side, it's American. Driving dark roads in the new hours of a new year, they could be any conventional couple on their way home from somewhere. Yet who but the two inside in the dim green glow of the dash know the roads they've already driven or the ones they've yet to drive, understand the particular routes that brought them to this exact stretch of curve at this hour on this night, believe, as one among them is determined to, that what's up ahead in a few days time might bring them back to where they started all those years ago.

A stretch of curve and we hit ice, skidding quick, wheel lock, fishtail, lights, stone wall, trees trees "watch out Dan Dan Dan God Almighty slow down" a jag, then studs grab, and it's good road again. You breathe from the ground up.

"Jesus, that's all we need is to die now." My pulse, my pulse, my pulse. "God." My pulse.

To the road: "All right now, all right?"

To the speedometer: "All right."

To the dark beyond the headlights: "All right."

His hands on the wheel, locked, like he'll never take them off.

I hate winter driving. I hate it.

Good Hill Extension.

Eastly Road.

Pink Cloud Lane.

Home.

TEN

Beyond words.

GOD, WEEP TEARS OF REPENTANCE FOR WHAT YOU
do in the night when no one is looking. And shame be
yours for the moonlit trick you pulled on a household on
a hill down a lane in a town in the woods.

———·———

Pick a date out of thin air, pick it like a Bingo number:
January 4th. Circle it on the bank's new calendar hanging
by the kitchen phone; ring it in DoctorRed so all who see
it know the new year starts with a bang. Give it a moment
to do handstands and cartwheels on the braided rug in
the playroom, birthday-party happy let it leap into hearts
and affix itself there with Super Glue. It's a date out of
any thousand, a Sunday out of any thousand, but imbue

that any-Sunday out of thousands with an unrealistic weight: The Un-Doing Day. Make it The Day that will un-do what should never have been done.

Set the table for a Saturday supper of steak and potatoes and salad and bread and blood red beans. Such a bounty of vitamins and riboflavins and complex carbohydrates to fuel the future. It's a Saturday supper like any Saturday supper, but tonight, don't let us have dessert until we swallow every bite.

Fill our hearts with hope, will you? Offer it up with bedtime glasses of milk irradiated to not turn sour before lips touch rims. Toss us hopeful in our sleep, knees and shoulders drawn in fetal bliss, happy-baby dreams under warm blankets, soft wool blankets tucked tight with hospital corners.

Send a wife and children to bed on a Saturday night snuggling the belief that tomorrow the years will start to reverse. Starting tomorrow, the dials on the X-ray machine that turned to the right twenty years ago will U-turn left. The levers that clicked up the wattage and scrambled a man's circuits will click back down to human levels. And the lead pad that stayed folded in a cupboard, or was it hanging from a hook behind the door, either or, that lead pad unfolded will tomorrow transform into a magic carpet, a magic lead carpet on which the future will ride.

Then send a man to sleep on a Saturday night, a Saturday night that could be any Saturday night. Send him to sleep ambivalent about the day to come and the one to come after and the news that both might bring. Lay his heavy body down on his son's carpeted floor to give the ache in his back a reprieve, carpeting green as grass that might have served his younger self on a spring day a place to nap and dream of dreams to come. Send him to sleep ambivalent at one end of a long house while his wife dreams of certainties at the other, wills her dreams to certainties on her half of their brass bed. Send him to sleep alone on a floor on a Saturday night he doesn't want to treat as anything special. Crank his snores, crackle his breathing as you have on every other night, clog him, cork him, and then let his ambivalence choke his heart.

Like that.

In the night.

On a cold night that could be any Saturday night, half dressed and unblanketed on a floor in a room alone, write him off.

———

The colors of his life were not vibrant, but in the moment of his death make him art. Stipple his face with the shadows of moon-stained clouds racing overhead, tipple them down through a skylight in the vaulted ceiling of his son's bedroom and wash them vertical across his setting cheeks. And the beads of night sweat on his empty scalp: before they dry turn them to diamonds with pops of moonlight. He is a mountain range rising from a verdant base, his landscape snowcapped in the nightglow, flecked with mica, still and eternal, big brother to the boulder in his yard. He is a holy icon, radiant with an inner glory, arms outstretched to anybody's guess as he stiffens on his back, Christ-like as any Jewish man could be. He is shape and color pure, form for form's sake, all line and space and dimension. Then remember who you are, and who he is, and that the art of mercy is elective. And as the night breaks for day, make him no more captivating to the cultured and the critical than a dull child's chalk sketch on a sidewalk, unremarkable in concept and execution and easily washed away with a first rain. There are no witnesses other than you, and there will be nothing to document this one-night-only exhibition. But some of us have to believe that art is art, even when the lights are off.

He is not a successful man by any modern measure, not a leader, not a maverick, neither movie-star handsome nor magnetic in that way some people are who

draw looks from passersby just because. In business, on
the train, around his community, among the friends he
and his wife made because she made them he is not a
standout, and no one will say of him in years to come
if they even remember that they even remember him:
"Oh, that Dan, he was somethin', wudn' he?" If they remember him at all it will be because they remember her,
if they even remember her, the atomic blast and he, her
prince consort. He is one more man among millions and
millions, and as it is for the millions and millions before
him and will be for the millions and millions to follow
he will not be missed by those who never knew him. So
write him off.

Stop a man's breathing in the middle of the night, and
in a room two rooms away, let it be his oldest son, his
most sensitive son, who half wakes to hear what there
isn't to hear. Let that son in his half sleep lie still enough
to hear what there isn't to hear, but don't let him wake
enough to raise his head from the pillow to hear what
there isn't to hear all too silently. Do not let him wake
awake enough to take in the glow-in-the-dark hands
of the clock, to pull back the covers, to sit up and listen

the whole narrow length of his body to the sound of the dark. Do not let him wake awake enough to forego his slippers and his robe and make the cold night crossing from his carpeted floor to the cold wood in the hall to the stairs to the room where life no longer has volume. *As he should have,* he'll tell you; *why didn't he,* he'll wonder. Instead, let him spoon himself back asleep with what he heard or didn't hear a question to rattle in his dreams, one of several unanswered question to rattle in all his dreams for the rest of his life.

The end of a man's life, his last heartbeat, made no more noticeable to the sleeping than the air we breathe.

Like that.

In the night.

As the sun itself is just waking on the Sunday that's meant to be the Sunday of all Sundays, let that oldest son fold time and enact the scenario step-by-barefoot-step to find what was already too late to find when he didn't find it earlier. Let him live with the discovery quiet and alone in the still house, considerate of his younger brothers still asleep, of his mother asleep a length of house away. Let his arms hang off the discovery quiet and alone, but do not let them embrace himself, do not let them hug his own heart. While you're at it, do not bother giving his heart the need to be hugged; you have other plans for him, and feeling what he's never felt isn't among them, not yet.

He's the dutiful son, the competent one, the one most caught in the parental crossfire, so don't let him be a child who has lost his father, no don't. Keep him busy instead dialing the kitchen phone, and with each number drilling back in place give him an archeologist's focus to sift through the history of language from the first thoughtful grunt on up to find the words the living have always used to say what he now needs to say. These words, the first of his morning, he'll have to clear his throat to speak. With his free hand, he'll pantomime north and left and stop and hill as he gives directions to the ambulance dispatcher, his voice low and his tones even as the automaton takes over to fill in the blanks on their form: name, address, telephone number. Keep his steps soft and the phone within reach, all thinking, no feeling. This morning, the boy will learn what life isn't.

On this morning, at sixteen, the boy will find the

words to tell his mother that her husband is dead. He'll miss picking up the ringing telephone by a half tone, and half a house away the ringing will jar his mother awake and she will reach for it in her half sleep and tip the receiver to the ear that's not on her pillow and she will hear an unfamiliar voice asking for the age of "the deceased" and she will not understand why a more familiar voice is answering "fifty-seven." "Who is this," she will say in last night's extra cigarettes' voice, "what are you talking about? Adam? Is that you?" And he will tell her, as the caller disconnects, as the strange voice becomes the dial tone's drone, as matter-of-factly as he can over the telephone half a house away her firstborn will say to his mother, "Mummy," low and even, all thinking, no feeling, "Daddy's dead."

Later, later you'll allow him to feel. Later, when he's leading the congregation in Kaddish for his father, saying it from memory because that is who he is, standing narrow and pale next to the Rabbi who's tan from sailing, standing on the bima in front of the closed casket in front of the congregation, you'll allow him to feel what he's never felt. Up there narrow and pale next to the tanned Rabbi take the boy out of the boy and convulse his body beyond davening, push the tears out of him so violent and plump his Hebrew will drown in them. You'll allow him then to feel what he's never felt, make his sadness look fresh as a new infection that can be cured, but it will already be too late to contain the grief. It wasn't attended to at the moment of contact, and now, no comfort will ever reach the marrow where it burrows deep for life-keeping. No palliative will ever find its way there. His eyes will always show it in the sag of their corners, his fine hands in their restlessness, the way his narrow body as it slumps through the years will retreat from even the most casual touch. In the full man to come, gloom will mull bone-deep, resistant to all ministrations, and the small bit of boy that's left in him will abandon archeology and no longer dig for the words to explain exactly why.

In the kitchen, the youngest will be at his oldest brother's elbow in time for the words to enter the world. Sleep still on his body as extra pajamas, and his pajamas not yet cold from uncovering, this bean of a boy will catch the words as sparks from a fire. The smoke and flames not real to him until he watches his brother return the receiver to the wall phone, hook it carefully into place like a fact, both hands on it and staying there, even as he turns his face so their eyes can connect.

"He's . . . ?"

"Yes."

Half a house away, a spark not so composed, this one fighting with its slippers and the arms of its robe, will ignite their brother from sleep, their brother who slept on their father's side of their parents' bed, slept there sound if resentful not to be in his own bed, not in his own bed in his own room because in his room on his floor their father was asleep, and their father's snoring can wake the dead.

———

The telephone bell will have rung early on a Sunday morning that was meant to be the Sunday of all Sundays and a wife will have started her morning prepared for the wrong day. Asleep like her children on the prayer that, come today, a doctor ex machina will fix everything, wake her instead to an empty station platform and the dream she thought she could will to life a missed train speeding away and fading around the bend. In her hand, the train schedule, in red and white the towns and the trains and their times, and by her train an asterisk denoting it an express bypassing all the stops that have slowed them in the past and shooting them straight to the promised land, and here she was dressed and on the platform with her ticket already purchased, and all for naught.

Blow horns in her head, loud ones. Blare the irony of his death cacophonous. "He wasn't any more sick than usual he was finally going to a doctor he was fine last night he was OK how could this what the why . . . ?" Remind her of the night, and the morning, and the co-incidence of the future so close, and set the base notes for the recurring phrase that will play for all time as a question that will never be answered.

———

Married for seventeen years to a man she slept with for twenty-one, twenty of them spent speculating how many years he had left in him and how many they would have together and how many years her sons would have with their father, stacking the counts on a shelf with every new pair of shoes, every new job, every dollar salted away for her children's educations and the num-ber seems small. Smaller with the arrival of concerned friends, concern arriving in pairs, and, later in the day, more pairs of relatives who clog her driveway with their out-of-state plates and lengthy marriages. Thirty-six years. Forty-nine years. Numbers she will never know.

Smaller as her own uncelebrated anniversaries mount in the years to come, uncelebrated but milestones all the same until the number of years she's a widow is almost twice what she was a wife.

And sooner for her sons the number of years fatherless. Boys they are, one just sixteen, one a month away from thirteen and his Bar Mitzvah, the youngest not yet eleven but his birthday's almost here. Will they become the men they might have become without the man they've lost? It will take her hours and days and weeks and months of clinging to the shock of having lost her husband before she finds her reading glasses, and rests them low on her nose as is her wont, and sees that her sons have lost their father. But once she does, and for all the years to come of sleepless nights wherein her regret will keep her awake for not having acknowledged their loss as profoundly as her own, she will become extra vigilant, peeling her eyes for signs, as their bodies inch to completion and their faces take on the stubble of men, that they, too, have counted the years. Counted them and done their counts again, shifted the figures from the left column to the right and back, reconciled the debits and assets of his having died when he did as she herself has done, recounted them with every recurring downbeat from the horns forever in her head. The numbers and the notes phrasing the same question about their father, her husband, about the night, and the morning, and the coincidence of his death, the irony of his not living past the eve of the future. The same question having gone unanswered among his sons as well as his wife: *Would it have made any difference? Would it have made any difference? Would it have made any difference?*

But on this Sunday morning that was meant to be the Sunday of all Sundays, a morning not of ambulances and hearses but golden chariots, on through burying her husband twenty-four hours later, at her oldest son's insistence of orthodox tradition, on the Monday morning that was meant to be an as-important-as-Sunday Monday with its diagnostics and diagnoses, and on through seven days of black crepe over every mirror including the one at her makeup vanity, mercifully over her vanity so she cannot see how forty-seven is looking on her now, the knife behind her eyes slicing all the way down into her heart isn't the unknown, it's the familiar, and what she wants is what she had, back.

———

Nude and delusional on her own January deathbed, fighting the hold of her hand by her youngest son, her youngest who's not yet forty but his birthday's almost here, the past is her morphine, and the drips its resurrection.

Twenty-nine years is an hour, is a season. She can try them for fit as she might her favorite old fashions, fashions kept fresh with camphor balls in the garment bags in the attic of her house, the house in the woods she hasn't gone to for years. They wear her as she did them the years after he died, Ultrasuede and maxicoats and pantsuits and faux-fur, adapting to each other's changing hemlines and hues as she did to widowhood. Trying them on as she did other men, studying their drape in a three-panel mirror, how they fit her hips, her arms, her heart, the years, but deciding in the end that the look was simply too young for her. Wardrobe after wardrobe, until she no longer wore hats, and let the blood drain from her obsession with Red to all things Coral.

Twenty-nine years is an hour, is an ad. The run-on sentences that were her married life reduced to the three-word headline and the brief, broad stroke of smart body copy. Hedge after high-paying hedge against uncertainty with the money itself the end that meant all, though she's loathe to look at her work portfolio for the holes she sees in it, seeing not the career others would in a single signature line. *"Share the Fantasy"* was hers, written riding a dirty bus on a muggy day, recalling a memory of a memory of a feeling from a long-ago time when immortality was hers, when a younger self under a long-gone sun had it in her to live forever. Invoice after freelance invoice until her sagging body bad-mouthed her ever-vital mind, and the life she had down letter-perfect let her down.

Twenty-nine years is an hour, is a life, is a house, is a tree, is a train, is a car, is a dog, is a dress, is a baby, is a tie, is a neighbor, is a Nettie, is a dream. A melancholy dream, ephemeral and free-floating between herself and the son by her side, an FM-radio transmission, more than one, of hard news and sad music from way back when coming through to him loud and clear.

Tell Dan: the Swoons got divorced.

Tell Dan: Nixon was a crook.

Tell Dan: the Waxlers got divorced.

Tell Dan: they ended Vietnam.

Tell Dan: Evelyn Lenz got remarried. And divorced.

Tell Dan: they lowered the speed limit to 55.

Tell Dan: Mary Fence committed suicide.

Tell Dan: I've taken an apartment in the city.

Tell Dan: fur is dead.

Tell Dan: Elvis is still alive.

Tell Dan: they found the Titanic.

Tell Dan: do do that voodoo that you do so well.

Tell Dan: the Berlin Wall came down.

Tell Dan: they're handing out condoms at Eastly High School.

Tell Dan: they're talking of going to Mars.

Tell Dan: the house is for sale.

Tell Dan: he's a Grandfather.

Tell Dan: to wake up: it's time to go to the hospital.

Tell Dan: I'm coming.

———

January 1st, January 2nd, January 3rd. "Do you think she's holding out to die the same day he did?" "I don't know, Josh, I don't know. Ask Charlie." January 7th, January 8th, January 9th.

———

Daniel M. _____, 57, of Pink Cloud Lane, Eastly, died early Sunday morning, January 4th, of causes unknown. He leaves behind a wife and three sons.

Daniel M. _____, 57, of Pink Cloud Lane, Eastly, died out of the blue early Sunday morning, January 4th, the Sunday that was meant to be the day his life would begin anew twenty-nine years ago and left behind a wife who wasn't prepared for him to die, in spite of the years she had spent wondering when and how he would, left behind three sons who would grow to men with more of her in them than him, three sons who never met the man he was before he was the man they knew, left behind a blank space where his big, sick body use to be, a space filled in with the moss of time and distraction, filled in and covered over six feet deep, mourned for until the memory faded, and was forgotten, and it was he who was left behind.

Until, nude and delusional on her own January death-bed, his wife exhumes the ghost of him, breathing him out into the room with the very life left in her. Bringing the life of him to life, and the loss of him to life, and her love for him to life with short, pale, shallow breaths, quiet breaths, in the early hours of a new morning. And the hand fighting the hand holding hers, the fight in it fades. And her hand is calm in the hand holding hers, her son's hand, her youngest son's hand. Her hand is calm in his, calm and resigned to letting go, holding onto her child in a way she never has.

The warm in it waning. The warm in it gone. Like

that. In the night. Gone but for a faint buzz of current beneath her flesh, the faint buzz of current that unites us all. And we are all in the room. Dan and Myrmy and Adam and Charlie and me, and Nettie and Aggie and the babies. And it's a spring day with the top down in a car on a country road on the way to a house in the woods.

Suggested Topics for Discussion

1. Myrmy and Dan take turns narrating the story of their marriage. What would change if only Myrmy or only Dan (but not both) told their story? What is gained when two people tell the same story? If someone other than you or your spouse were to tell your story, what kinds of details would they miss? What would they be able to add?

2. Discuss the sacrifices that Myrmy and Dan make in order to build and maintain their marriage. Do you think their differences prevent them from being happy? How are the shortcomings of each compensated in other ways?

3. Discuss Myrmy's conversation with the real estate agent. Why does the agent decline to offer her services at first? How did Myrmy find the agent? How does the nature of the conversation change when the agent accidentally tells Myrmy about her problems with pregnancy?

4. In families with two working parents, children usually spend a significant amount of time with childcare workers. How do Myrmy and Dan interact with their

children? How does the role of their nanny add or detract from their role as parents? How do childcare workers take part in family life? Who ultimately makes choices for the children; the parents or the childcare? Does the active role played by childcare workers change the modern definition of a family?

5. This book takes place at a time when women were just beginning to be hired for high-powered positions. How does Myrmy's career affect her relationships with the women in her life? How does it affect her self-image?

6. Dan seems to suffer from a mysterious disease that affects his mental and physical health. What causes him to change from a physically fit Army man to an overweight tie salesman with a heart problem? Does Myrmy's high-powered job threaten him? Or is he suffering from something in his past?

7. There are times when Myrmy and Dan don't seem to know, or even like, the other person. Is it possible to truly ever "know" another person?

ROBERT HILL grew up in Connecticut, received a BA in Literature from Boston University, and lives in Portland, Oregon. He has been an advertising copywriter, a grant writer, and a teaching fellow at the Bread Loaf Writers' Conference. *When All Is Said and Done* is his first novel.

When All Is Said and Done has been set in Adobe Caslon Pro, an open type version of a typeface originally designed by William Caslon sometime between 1720 and 1766. The Adobe version was drawn by Carol Twombly in 1989.

Book design by Wendy Holdman.
Manufactured by Versa Press on acid-free paper.